KING ARTUS

Medieval Studies

Mary Maleski *and* Jo Ann McNamara, *Series Editors*

KING ARTUS

A Hebrew Arthurian Romance of 1279

Edited and Translated with Cultural
and Historic Commentary by

Curt Leviant

SYRACUSE UNIVERSITY PRESS

First Syracuse University Press Edition 2003
03 04 05 06 07 08   6 5 4 3 2 1

Originally published in 1969 by Ktav Publishing House.
Reprinted by arrangement with the author.

The paper used in this publication meets the minimum requirements
of American National Standard for Information Sciences—Permanence
of Paper for Printed Library Materials, ANSI Z39.48–1984.∞™

Library of Congress Cataloging-in-Publication Data
Melech Artus. English & Hebrew
King Artus : a Hebrew Arthurian romance of 1279 / edited and
translated with cultural and historic Commentary by Curt Leviant.— 1st
Syracuse University Press ed.
p. cm.—(Medieval studies)
Includes bibliographical references.
ISBN 0–8156–3011–5
1. Arthurian romances. 2. Merlin (Legendary
character)—Romances. 3. Romances, Hebrew—Translations
into English. I. Leviant, Curt. II. Title. III. Series.
PJ5050 .K53 2003
892.4'32—dc21   2003012230

Manufactured in the United States of America

And Yseult was fair and lovely to behold.
—from a medieval Tristan and Yseult romance

To my cousins
Kalman and Riva Leviant
scions and supporters of learning and piety

Curt Leviant is the author of five widely praised novels, *The Yemenite Girl, Passion in the Desert, The Man Who Thought He Was Messiah, Partita in Venice,* and *Diary of an Adulterous Woman,* the last published by Syracuse University Press. He has also translated and edited twenty other books, including a dozen translations of fiction by Sholem Aleichem, Chaim Grade, Avraham Reisen, and Isaac Bashevis Singer. His most recent work of translation, Eliezer Shtaynbarg's *Jewish Book of Fables,* was also published by Syracuse University Press in 2003. Mr. Leviant has won several literary prizes and major national and international writing fellowships for his fiction and translations.

Contents

Acknowledgments

It is a pleasure to acknowledge my thanks to Sara Mandelman of Jerusalem, Israel, for her kind assistance and comments in reference to the materials in Old French. And to my wife, Erika Leah, my heartfelt gratitude for her constant encouragement and keen perspicacity.

KING ARTUS

1

General Introduction to
the Hebrew Arthurian Romance

A. *Previous Scholarship*

A most unique work in Hebrew literature is a thirteenth century Hebrew translation of an Arthurian romance.[1] Although this intriguing ms., the only one of its kind extant, should presumably be of interest to scholars in Arthurian and in Hebraic studies, it has been rather neglected. Aside from an edition published eighty years ago, two brief articles, and an English translation, no study has been devoted to the Hebrew Romance.

First to call attention to the Hebrew Romance was Abraham Berliner, who transcribed it from the unique copy at the Vatican Library and published his recension in *Otzar Tob*, in 1885,[2] but without explanatory material or critical apparatus. In a one-paragraph introduction he states that he has no reason to doubt that 1279 is the date of the ms. – the date which the scribe himself provided in the first line of his composition – and adds that he has no other Arthurian texts before him with which to compare the Hebrew Romance.[3]

Comparing the Vatican ms. with Berliner's recension will reveal that in the latter are added words, alterations in orthography, substitution of one word for another, omission of words and phrases, and a variety of misreadings, all of which have been corrected in

---

[1] Since the ms. is untitled, I will refer to it as the Hebrew Romance.

[2] *Otzar Tob*, Berlin, 1885, pp. 1-11. This was published as a Hebrew supplement to the periodical listed immediately below.

[3] *Magazine f. d. Wissenschaft d. Judenthums*, Berlin, 1885, p. 225.

the present edition. No doubt many of the discrepancies between the ms. and Berliner can be ascribed to typographical errors. Nevertheless, all the succeeding comments on the ms. were based upon the printed version.

Next to deal with the Hebrew romance was the noted Jewish bibliographer, Moritz Steinschneider, whose approach is slightly more detailed and analytic than Berliner's.[4] Writing in German, Steinschneider gives a reader unfamiliar with Hebrew an opportunity to apprehend the contents of the romance and estimate its significance. He labels the untitled ms. *Melech Artus* (King Artus), provides the bibliographical information concerning the Berliner edition, and then summarizes the thirteenth century scribe's apology and text.[5] Steinschneider considers that the length of the apology indicates the scribe's awareness of the new matter he was bringing into the sacred language. Since "Verherrlichung der rohen Muskelkraft," bloody chivalry and the tales concerning figures involved in adultery could find no advocates in Judaism, Steinschneider views this translation as one of the greatest curiosities in Hebrew literature.[6] On the basis of several Italian words in the text, Steinschneider concludes that the Hebrew translator worked from an Italian original.[7]

A fuller treatment of the romance was offered by M. Schuler in 1909.[8] The article, which is also based on Berliner's printed version, reviews the remarks of Berliner and Steinschneider, and then summarizes the apology and the text.

Schuler's contribution is his citation of Old French romances as the source from which the two stories in the Hebrew romance are ultimately, but not immediately, derived. The first episode, containing the story of Uther Pendragon's seduction of Igraine with the aid of Merlin and the conception of Arthur, comes from the prose *Merlin*. The second story, describing Lancelot's love affair with King Arthur's wife, Guinevere, his trip to Winchester and his

---

[4] M. Steinschneider, *Hebraische Uebersetzungen*, Berlin, 1893, pp. 967-969.
[5] *Ibid.*, pp. 967-968.
[6] *Ibid.*, p. 968.
[7] *Ibid.*
[8] "Die hebraische Version der Sage von Arthur und Lanzelot aus dem Jahre 1279", M. Schuler, *Archiv f. neure Sprachen u. Lit.*, vol. cxxii, pp. 51-63.

2

meeting with the Maid of Askalot, and his jousts at the tournament, is drawn from the *Mort Artu*.[9]

At the opening of the Hebrew romance the scribe states that he has omitted about three pages from the book he was translating.[10] Schuler feels that this refers to the Lancelot story since the many omissions and condensations in the Uther story come to more than three pages. Moreover, the scholar continues, the dissimilarities between the Uther story in Hebrew and in French show that the Hebrew scribe did not consider this first story essential and therefore relied on memory.[11]

Schuler feels that, whereas the first story of the Hebrew Romance does not closely follow its ultimate Old French source, the prose *Merlin*, the Lancelot episode does bear close resemblance to the *Mort Artu*. In support of this view, Schuler cites two brief passages in O.F., the opening of the Lancelot fragment[12] and one battle scene from the tournament at Winchester.[13] Since no German text of the Hebrew Romance was available to the reader, Schuler summarizes the entire romance.[14]

On the basis of the Italian words in the Hebrew text, Schuler asserts that the Hebrew translator's immediate source was an Italian version of some Arthurian legends.[15] The form of the Italian words in the text indicates to Schuler that the Hebrew scribe wrote in Northern Italy, probably Tuscany.[16] The fact of a Hebrew Arthurian romance of 1279 in Italy, Schuler concludes, points to the

---

[9] Schuler, p. 53. The differences between the Hebrew and the O. F. will be discussed below in chapter 6.

[10] See Translation, p. 9. Schuler's argument is based on the fact that the Uther episode, which takes up two pages in the Hebrew text, has many more pages in French. For instance, in Sommer's edition, the same events are printed in eighteen folio-size pages. See *Vulgate Version of the Arthurian Romance*, ed. H. O. Sommer, Washington, vol. ii, pp. 58-76.

[11] Schuler, p. 53.   [12] *Ibid.*, p. 55.

[13] *Ibid.*, pp. 58-59.   [14] *Ibid.*, pp. 59-60.

[15] *Ibid.*, p. 62.

[16] *Ibid.*, p. 63. Two noted contemporary Romance language scholars agree with Schuler. After examining the Italian words and names in the Hebrew romance, they feel that the scribe probably lived in Northern Italy. Letters of Mario Pei of Columbia University, dated Feb. 6, 1965, and Joseph M. Barrone of Princeton University, dated Feb. 2, 1965.

existence of a now lost Italian prose romance in the last quarter of the thirteenth century.[17]

Moses Gaster's translation of Berliner's edited text was the first of the romance into a modern language.[18] In his preface Gaster provides bibliographical information concerning Berliner's edition and summarizes the findings of Steinschneider and Schuler.[19] Gaster states that the Hebrew translation was undoubtedly made from a prose and not a metrical romance, and is ultimately based upon a French text.[20]

Although Gaster is an excellent translator, his version of the Hebrew romance must be considered inaccurate, for it is based upon an imprecise printed edition which does not correctly reflect the ms. Moreover, Gaster's translation neglects the biblical nuances, tones down the sexual elements, and condenses some lines. Schuler's article, the only scholarly treatment of the Hebrew romance, and Gaster's English translation appeared during the first decade of this century. Aside from some passing references in footnotes, the subject seems to have been forgotten.[21]

B. *The Manuscript*

The purpose in presenting a new edition of the Hebrew Arthurian Romance of 1279 is to make available in one study the Hebrew text, based upon a personal examination of the ms., and an English translation with explanatory notes and background material. Only one copy of this ms. exists and it is found in the Vatican Library.[22]

---

[17] Cf. J. D. Bruce, *Evolution of the Arthurian Romance*, p. 294, n. 2. Bruce is evidently familiar with the Hebrew romance (presumably Gaster's translation), for he states that "an Italian version (now lost) of the *Mort Artu* appears to have been in existence as early as 1279."

[18] M. Gaster, "The History of the Destruction of the Round Table as told in Hebrew in 1279", *Folklore*, vol. xx (1909), pp. 272-294.

[19] *Ibid.*, pp. 272-274.

[20] *Ibid.*, p. 275.

[21] Bruce, *op. cit.*, p. 294, n. 2, and Loomis, *Arthurian Literature in the Middle Ages*, p. 419, where Gaster is erroneously cited as the author of Schuler's article.

[22] Cod. Vat. Hebr. Urbino 48, ff. 75-77.

Except for a few greyish spots, which may have been caused by age, the vellum is excellently preserved. The ms. occupies four folios and a part of a fifth, each of which measures $10\frac{3}{4}$ by $7\frac{3}{4}$ inches. One-inch margins border each side and the number of lines per full page of the small, closely-written script ranges from fifty to fifty-two. Most of the fifth folio is blank, except for thirteen lines at the top, at which point the scribe ceased his work, in mid-paragraph.[23] The incomplete presentation is puzzling, especially in view of the scribe's intention to render the entire *Mort Artu*.[24]

The date of the translation is given at the beginning of the ms. as 1279.[25] None of the authorities who have dealt with the text have seen any reason to doubt this date. The figure 1279 does not actually appear in Arabic numerals, but a proper interpretation of the two Hebrew letters (*lamed* and *tet*) according to the Hebraic system of dating yields 1279.[26]

Schuler and Steinschneider pointed out several Italian words in the Hebrew text and concluded that the scribe's immediate source was an Italian version of an Arthurian romance.[27] Additional evidence can be adduced to support this contention.

The first is an Italian word, *capperone* (hood), which appears toward the end of the ms.[28] The previous commentators did not see this word, for it appeared in the Berliner edition as *capidon*, presumably a misprint, since in Hebrew script the orthographically similar *daled* (d) and *resh* (r) can easily be misread. However, the more significant proof for an Italian source is the gloss in the top right-hand margin at the beginning of the ms, alongside the first line.[29] Since Berliner did not include this gloss in his text, none of the subsequent commentators were aware of its existence. This only gloss in the entire ms. consists of two words in Hebrew characters: the first is transliterated from Italian, *l'distruzion*; the second is a Hebrew word, *b'laaz*, which means "in the vernacular." The gloss is intended for the word *shmad* (destruction), which appears in the

---

[23] See Translation, p. 49.   [24] *Ibid.*, pp. 13, 23 & 29.
[25] *Ibid.*, p. 9.   [26] *Ibid.*, see detailed explanation in n. 2.
[27] They listed such words as *elmo, valvasor, cusini, iermani, pennon, scudier* and such names as *Bano* and *Wincestri*. See Schuler, p. 62 and Steinschneider, p. 968.
[28] See Translation, p. 45.   [29] *Ibid.*, p. 9.

opening sentence of the ms.: "This is the book of the destruction of King Artus' Round Table..." Evidently because of the multiple meanings of the word *shmad*,[30] the scribe glossed the word and informed the Italian-Jewish reader that in the vernacular from which he is translating, the word reads *l'distruzion*, and that the reader should understand the phrase in the first line to mean "destruction" and not "persecution" or "religious apostasy" of the Round Table. But despite this evidence which seems to point to an Italian version, now lost, as the scribe's immediate source, the Hebrew text rests ultimately upon the Old French prose *Merlin* and the *Mort Artu*, from which the Uther Pendragon and the Lancelot episodes are derived.[31]

We know nothing of the anonymous Hebrew translator. Since the work is unfinished, there is no colophon to provide information. However, the ms. tells us something about the scribe's education and reading. He was clearly well acquainted with the Bible, as is evidenced by the many quotations in the text. He also knew Mishna and Talmud, which he quotes in his apology, and was no doubt a pious Jew who, like his Italian-Jewish contemporaries, received both Jewish and secular training.

The scribe may also have been familiar with two thirteenth century Hebrew works, one that could be classified as secular, the other as sacred. In describing R. Johanan ben Zakkai's knowledge of fox fables, the scribe does not utilize the talmudic term for "fox fables," *mishlot shualim*, but writes instead *mishley shualim*. Since the latter phrase is the title of a thirteenth century collection of animal fables by Berakya ha-Nakdan, the scribe may either have read or known of this work.[32] The scribe may also have been familiar with the *Yalkut Shimoni*, a thirteenth century aggadic collection which lists the same exegesis to the biblical verse "And now bring on the minstrel" as does the Talmud.[33]

[30] Shmad can also mean "apostasy "and "religious persecution", as well as "destruction".

[31] A more detailed comparison of the Hebrew with the French is included in a separate chapter below.

[32] See Berakya ha-Nakdan, *Mishley Shualim*, ed. A. M. Haberman, Tel Aviv, 1946.

[33] See Translation, p. 11, and *Yalkut Shimoni*, Berlin, 1926, p. 762.

As for non-Hebraic literature, it can be stated with certainty that the scribe knew more of romance than his translation indicates at first glance. Although only a part of the Lancelot story appears in the Hebrew text which we possess,[34] the scribe was evidently familiar with the entire *Mort Artu* and intended to present the whole romance to his readers. The scribe also gives the title of a book concerning the grail quest: *Libro di la Kesta del Sangraal*.[35] Determining his familiarity with such a book is difficult, for he may have copied the title from his Italian source, or if not, then he was familiar either with the work itself or at least the title. In any case, a specific name for a book about the quest does not appear in the O.F. passage where Arthur orders a written account of the adventure.[36]

In addition to presenting the Hebrew text with an English translation on facing pages to facilitate comparison, the following chapters will also attempt to relate the Hebrew Romance to the tradition of Hebrew letters and literary taste during the thirteenth century, and show why and how the Arthurian romance was not only translated into Hebrew, but in the process was also judaized and transformed. As a corollary to the Jewish aspects of the Hebrew Romance, Jewish parallels to some Arthurian motifs in the entire Arthurian tradition will also be presented. Finally, the episodes in the Hebrew Romance will be compared to like sections in the O.F. romances, in order to examine the scribe's attitudes to his source from a literary and a religio-cultural point of view.

The lettered footnotes in the Hebrew refer to biblical passages. The translation of biblical passages generally follows the version of the Jewish Publication Society's English edition of the Holy Scriptures. Departures from the J.P.S. translation will be noted as they occur.

The following symbols are used in the Hebrew text:

// - emandation
( ) - deletion
|| - completed abbreviation

The bracketed numbers within the Hebrew text correspond to the folio numbers of the manuscript.

---

[34] The ms. breaks off in the middle of the tournament at Winchester.
[35] See Translation, p. 25.   [36] See *Mort Artu, op. cit.*, pp. 1-2.

7

לדשטרוציאן
בלעז

[75] זה ספר השמד הטבלה העגולה שלהמלך ארטוש ואני העתקתיו בשנת
ט״ל לפרט מלשון לעז אל לשון עברי. ובהעתיקי אותו דילגתי קצת דברים
שהיו בספר שהועתק זה ממנו. ועשיתי כן בעבור שאותם העניינים הם רק
דברי שאילות ותשובות איש לרעהו או קינות או דברי גררות באו במקרה
ואינם מעצם הסיפור ולכן דילגתים. והם דברים מעטים שלא יעלו בין כולם
לסכום ג׳ דפין קטנים.

והשתדלתי בהעתקת אלה השיחות לשתי סיבות גדולות. הראשונה היתה על
דרך שמירת בריאות גופי כי בעוגנותיי רבו צרותיי ועצמו אנחותיי והנני שקוע
בנבכי ים המחשבות יושב ותוהה עומד ומשתומם על קורותיי ימים ולילות
ויראתי פן אפול בחולי השחורה שהוא חולי השטות אשר טוב ממנו המות.

8

2

Hebrew Text and Translation

(L'DISTRUZION)
The destruction
in the vernacular[1]

This is the book of the destruction of King Artus' Round Table and I have translated it from the vernacular into Hebrew in the year 39.[2] While translating, I omitted some passages which were in the book from which this translation was made. I did this because these passages contained only questions and answers between one person and another, or elegies, or irrelevant matters which were not pertinent to the story itself. Therefore I omitted them, for they were insignificant and did not even add up to three small leaves.

I attempted the translation of these conversations for two important reasons. The first was the preservation of my physical well-being, for owing to my sins my troubles have grown and my laments increased, and I am immersed in a sea of perplexed thoughts. Night and day I am continually astounded by events which have passed over me and I fear lest I fall into melancholy, that is madness, to

---

[1] See Intro., p. 5.

[2] Instead of numbers the text actually has two Hebrew letters – *lamed* (1) and *tet* (t). In addition to the Arabic system of numerals, the Hebrew uses another method of numeration whereby each letter of the alphabet has a certain value. Thus the first letter *aleph* is one, the ninth letter *tet* is nine, the tenth letter *yod* is ten. Thereafter the letters have decimal values. *Kaf* is twenty, *lamed* thirty. In our text, the combination of *lamed-tet* equals 39. The year 39 is meaningless unless we add 5000, a figure which is rarely written. To reckon the date according to the Christian calendar, one must subtract 3760 from the Hebrew year: 5039-3760 = 1279, the date of the Hebrew manuscript.

ולכן העתקתי לעצמי אלה השיחות כדי להעביר בהם זמני הרע בקצת
העתים ולהפיס דעתי ולהפיג צערי. ואין לשום משכיל שירנין עלי בזה כי
הנה ראינו לקצת מרבותינו ע״ה כמו רבן יוחנן בן זכאי שלא מנע עצמו
מידיעת משלי שועלים ומשלי כובסים ושיחות דקל/י/מ^א. וזה בעבור שיגיע
לאדם מידיעת אותם הסיפורים שום הפגה ושום הנחה אל הנפש העמלה
בעיסקי תורה או בעיסקי דרך ארץ.

וכן אמ|ר| הנביא ועתה קחו לי מנגן וכו'^ב ורבותינו ע״ה דרשו על זה מה
שידעת. ועוד כי א(י)פשר ללמוד מהם חכמה ומוסר בהנהגת האדם את עצמו
ואת זולתו. ולכן אינם שיחות בטלות ולא שיחות חולין. והראיה על זה היא
שאם היו שיחות חולין לא למדם רבי יוחנן בן זכאי בשכבר העידו אמרו
עליו על רבי יוחנן בן זכאי שמימיו לא שח שיחת חולין^ג.

א[.] בבא בתרה קלד,א: אמרו עליו על רבן יוחנן בו זכאי שלא הניח מקרא ומשנה...
ומשלות כובסים ומשלות שועלים שיחת שדים ושיחת דקלים.
ב[.] מלכים־ב ג,טו.
ג[.] סוכה כח,א: אמרו עליו על רבן יוחנן בן זכאי מימיו לא שח שיחת חולין ולא
הלך ד' אמות בלא תורה.

which death is preferable. Therefore I have translated these con- *[intent of translating]*
versations for myself in order to calm my mind, mitigate my grief,
and dispel somewhat the bad times I have experienced.

No intelligent person can rebuke me for this, for we have seen that
some of our sages of blessed memory, such as Rabbi Johanan ben
Zakkai,[3] did not disdain the knowledge of fox-fables, washers'
parables or the speech of palm trees.[4] And this is done so that a man
who is steeped in Torah-study or in worldly pursuits may derive
from the knowledge of these tales a measure of relaxation and relief. *[Hebrew Bible]*

Thus the prophet[5] said: "And now bring on the minstrel,"[6] and *[Babylon-ian Talmud]*
our sages interpreted this, as you well know.[7] Moreover, it is possible
to learn wisdom and ethics from these fables concerning a man's
conduct toward himself and towards his fellow man. Therefore they
are neither idle nor profane talk. The proof for this is that had they
been profane talk Rabbi Johanan ben Zakkai would not have
studied them. For it is said concerning Rabbi Johanan that during
his entire lifetime he never uttered profane talk.[8] *Hmm*

---

[3] Johanan ben Zakkai, a scholar of the first century C.E., was responsible for
the spiritual recovery of Israel after the destruction of the Temple in the
year 70. After founding a school at Jabneh to continue the chain of tradition
and learning, he reconstituted the Sanhedrin, the supreme court, which super-
vised religious law as well as civil and criminal jurisprudence. See Max
Margolies and Alexander Marx, *A History of the Jewish People*, Philadelphia,
1956, p. 205, and Baron, II, p. 277.

[4] Babylonian Talmud (B. T.), Tractate Baba Batra 134a. "It was said of
R. Johanan ben Zakkai that his studies included the Scriptures, the Mishna
...washers' proverbs, fox fables, and the speech of palm trees." Fox fables
were widespread in Talmudic times. (Rabbi Johanan said: "Rabbi Meir had
three hundred fox fables; we have only three left." B.T., Sanhedrin 38b.)

[5] Elisha.

[6] II Kings 3:15.

[7] B.T., Tractate Pesachim 66b. Our thirteenth century scribe points out that
diversion may lead to higher sacred accomplishment and cites a rabbinic
commentary as proof. The gist of the commentary on this verse is that the
power of prophecy was restored to Elisha after the minstrel had begun to
play. The same exegesis is quoted in *Yalkut Shimoni*, Berlin, 1926, p. 762,
a thirteenth century aggadic collection which the scribe may have been
familiar with. See also B.T., Sabbath 30b.

[8] B.T. Sukka 28a, "They said concerning R. Johanan ben Zakkai that during
his entire lifetime he never uttered profane talk, nor walked four cubits
without studying the Torah."

אם כן משמֹ|עֹ| מיכאן שאותם אינם שיחות חולין. ואלה הסיפורים שלזה
הספר שהעתקתי אינם פחותים ממשלי כובסים אדרבה הם מעולים ונכבדים
מהם עד מאד. עוד מצאנו שהיו מדברים לפני כהן גדול בלילי יום הכיפורים
שיחות מלכים קדמונים כדי שלא יישן ויעביד בהם את עתו כל הלילהא
כשהכהן לא היה בעל תורה אם כן אין ראוי להרחיקם.

הסיבה השנית אל העתקתי והיא הנכבדת היתה כי בתכלית שלזה הספר
ילמדו החוטאים דרכי התשובה ויזכרו אחריתם וישובו אל השם כמו שתראה
בסופו. ודיי בהתנצלותי זה אצל כל חכם מודה על האמת בלתי מקשה
עצמו לדעת.

אלה תולדותב מסיר לנצולוט. תדע כי המלך בנו מבנואיק והמלך בורז
מגאוניש היו אחים ונשאו שתי אחיות מזרע בית דוד.
והמלך בנו הוליד בן ונקרא שמו לנצולוט דללק. והסיבה למה נקרא דללק

<hr />

א· יומא א,ו–ז: אם היה חכם – דורש, ואם לאו – תלמידי חכמים דורשין לפניו; ואם
רגיל לקרות – קורא, ואם לאו – קורין לפניו. ובמה קורין לפניו? באיוב ובעזרא ובדברי
הימים. זכריה בן קביטל אומר: פעמים הרבה קריתי לפניו בדניאל. בקש להתנמנם
פרחי כהונה מכין לפניו באצבע צרדה, ואומרים לו: אישי כהן גדול, עמד והפג
אחת על הרצפה. ומעסיקין אותו עד שיגיע זמן השחיטה.
ב· השווה בר' ו:ט, יא:י אלה תולדות נח, אלה תולדות שם.

12

We can therefore conclude from this that these fables are not idle talk, and the stories which I have translated are no less worthy than the washers' parables; on the contrary, they are far more excellent and distinguished.

Moreover, we find that on the eve of the Day of Atonement the tales of ancient kings would be read to an unscholarly High Priest throughout the night so that he would not fall asleep.[9] Consequently, there is no need to shun them.

The second and most important reason for my translation was that sinners will learn the paths of repentance and bear in mind their end and will return to the Name,[10] as you will see at the conclusion.[11]

Cool!

This apology should satisfy any intelligent man who admits the truth and is not willfully obstinate.

This is the history[12] of Sir Lancelot. Know that King Bano of Benoic and King Borz of Gaunes were brothers; they married two sisters, scions of the House of David.[13] King Bano begat a son who was called Lancelot del Lac. The reason why he was called del Lac

[9] Mishna Yoma 1:6-7. "If he was a Sage he used to expound the Scriptures, and if not the disciples of the Sage used to expound before him. If he was versed in reading the Scriptures, he read, and if not they read before him. And from what did they read before him? Out of Job and Ezra and Chronicles. If he sought to slumber, young men of the priesthood would snap their middle finger before him and say to him, 'My lord High Priest, get up and drive away sleep this once by walking on the cold pavement.' And they used to divert him until the time of slaughtering drew near."

[10] I.e., the Lord. A pious Jew will not write out God's name, unless it is used in a sacred text. Instead, he utilizes the substitute, *ha-shem*, literally *the Name* [of God]. See Megillat Taanit 7, and B.T. Rosh Hashana 18b.

[11] Since for some undetermined reason the MS breaks off in the middle of a paragraph, the conclusion is lacking. See Introduction.

[12] In Hebrew *toldot*: literally "the generations of" – a typically biblical opening to an epic story. Cf. Genesis 6:9, 11:10, and so on. The biblical verses footnoted in this translation are more fully discussed in Chapter 4.

[13] Since the story begins by setting up the line of King David as the object of geneological distinction, a sympathetic note is struck at the outset for the reader in Hebrew. Despite the absence of a kingdom, Jewish leaders, such as Hillel, R. Gamaliel, and the Exilarchs of Babylonia, traced their descent from the House of David. See Margolis and Marx, p. 235, and Baron, II, p. 196.

הלא היא כתובה[א] בספרו.   וגם כן שם תמצא מתי נודע אליו שמו.

והיה לו אח אחד ממזר כלומ|ר| שהיה בן המלך באגו משרית אחת מיוחסת
ונקר|א| שמו אשטור דמ/ר/יש נמצא שהיה אשטור אחי מסיר לנצולוט מצד
האב.   והמלך בורז הוליד שני בנים שם האחד בורז כשם אביו ושם הש(י)ני
ליאונל.   נמצא שבורז וליאונל היו שניים כלו'|מר| קושיני יירמני אל מסיר
לנצולוט ואל אשטור.

סדר תולדות המלך ארטוש.   תדע כי בימי המלך אוטיר פנדרגון היה
במלכות לוגריש דוכוס אחד גדול שמו הדוכוס מטיל טומייל.   ולו אשה יפה
עד מאד שמה מרת איזרנא.
ויהי היום ויצו המלך אוטיר פנדרגון לעשות סיבוב גדול מאד מכל פרשי
לוגריש לפני עיר קמלוט.   וכל פרש ורוזן יביא את אשתו אל הסיבוב למען
יתגבר לבב הפרשים ולבב הגבירות יעלוז.   וכן עשו כל הפרשים.   גם הדוכוס

[א] הש' מלכים־א יא,מא, ויתר דברי שלמה...הלא הם כתובים...ראה גם
מלכים־א יד,כט;טו,כג;טז,כד.

is it not written[14] in the book concerning him? There you will also find when his name was made known to him.[15]

He had a bastard brother, the son of King Bano and a noble lady, who was called Estor de Ma[r]eis;[16] Estor, then, was a brother to Sir Lancelot on his father's side.

King Borz begat two sons. One was named after his father, the other was named Lionel. Borz and Lionel, then, were cousins, that is, *cusini iermani*,[17] to Sir Lancelot and Estor.

The history of[18] King Artus

Know that in the days of Uter Pendragon there was a great duke in the Kingdom of Logris called the Duke of Til Tomeil.[19] He had an exceedingly beautiful wife named Lady Izerna.[20] One day King Uter Pendragon ordered a very great tournament for all the knights of Logris by the city of Camelot. Each knight and duke had to bring his wife to the tourney to inspire the hearts of the knights and gladden the hearts of the women. All the knights did so.

The Duke of Titomeil[21] brought his wife, the Duchess, to that

[14] *Is it not written?* is the biblical manner of indicating crossreference. Cf. I Kings 11:41, "And the rest of the acts of Solomon... are they not written in the book of the acts of Solomon." Other instances of the use of this phrase abound. I Kings 14:29, 15:23, 16:24 refer to "the book of chronicles of the kings of Judah." I Kings 22:39, 15:31, 16:5, 22:46 refer to "the book of chronicles of the kings of Israel." In the Bible, then, there is a tradition of establishing the veracity of the historic statements by making reference to other books.

[15] In the prose *Lancelot*, to which the Hebrew scribe makes one other reference. See *infra*, p. 29. This episode is found in Sommer, III, p. 196.

[16] Although here the letter *R* is totally blackened, in other references to Mareis the name is clearly spelled. See *infra* p. 45.

[17] i.e., first cousins. The scribe has transliterated the Italian words in the Hebrew text, perhaps to clarify the relationship for Italian-Jewish readers.

[18] Lit., "the order of the generations of..."

[19] In O.F. this name appears as Tintaiol. See Sommer, II, p. 58.

[20] One would expect Igerna. However, this is undoubtedly an Italian variant. In the fourteenth century *Vita di Merlino*, Uter Pendragon loves a women named Izerla. See E. Gardner, *The Arthurian Legend in Italian Literature*, London, 1930, p. 196. Future references to this work will be abbreviated to "Gardner."

[21] The scribe seems to have been careless here, for he spelled the name Til Tomeil a few lines above. Such inconsistency is found only in one other place where he transliterates *vavasour* (p. 35) and the next time writes it *valvasour* (p. 37).

15

מטיטאמיל הביא את אשתו הדוכסית שם. ויש לך לדעת כי היו לזה הדוכוס
ד׳ בנות מן הדוכסית לא נראו כמוה(ם)/ן/ בכל המלכות בהדר וביופי. ויעשה
הסיבוב גדול וחזק עד מאד ויעש המלך משתה גדול לכל העמים והשרים[א].
וישא את עיניו אל יפי הדוכסית איזרנא ואש אהבתה נשקה בלבבו.

ויקרב להתחלות[ב] ולא יכול עוד הצפינו וישלח אליה גביעו גביע הזהב
על יד אחד משריו ויצוהו לאמר אליה את חשקו ותבערת אהבתו. והדברים
ארוכים. סוף דבר סיפרה אל הדוכוס בעלה את דברי המלך אוטיר
פנדרגון. וכשומעו פחד על אשתו וישכם בבקר ויצו את עבדיו לאסור את
סוסיו. וירכב הוא וכל פרשיו וחברתו עם הדוכסית ולא לקח רשות מן המלך.

וייגד למלך כי העלים את דרכו ויחר לו מאד וישלח לו לאמר שישוב אל
החצר עם הדוכסית לאלתר ואם לאו שיהיה חוץ משלומו. והדוכוס לעג לו
וישב אל ארצו ויבצר את כל ארצו ויחזק את כל כרכיו ומגדליו כי ידע
שהמלך יבוא עליו לצבא. וכמשלוש חדשים הזעיק המלך את כל צבאיו
לעלות לצבא על הדוכוס וילך ויצר עליו בקריה אחת בצורה[ג] שנשתגב בה.
והדוכסית היתה בקריה אחרת נשגבה[ד] עד מאד עם בנותיה ואמהותיה ופרשים
גיבורים עמה בקריה. והמלך חיזק המצור על הקריריה שהיה בה הדוכוס
ונלחם בה ימים רבים ולא שוה לו. ויקרא את מרלין ויאמר לו אנא אחי

א׳   מגלת אסתר ב,יח: ויעש המלך משתה גדול לכל שריו ועבדיו.

ב׳   שמואל־ב יג,ב: ויצר לאמנון להתחלות בעבור תמר אחותו.

ג׳   ישעיה כה,ב: כי שמת מעיר לגל קריה בצורה למפלה.

ד׳   ישעיה כו,ה: כי השח ישבי מרום קריה נשגבה.

16

place. Know that by this duchess the duke had four daughters, whose beauty and grace were unsurpassed in the entire kingdom.

The tournament proceeded mightily. Then the king made a great feast for all the people and all the princes.[22] He caught sight of the beauty of the Duchess Izerna and the flame of love was kindled in his heart. King ♡s Izerna
He became quite ill[23] and could no longer hide his love. So he sent her his golden cup through one of his officers. He ordered him to tell her of his desire and burning love. Now these matters are lengthy. Finally, however, she related Uter Pendragon's words to her husband, the Duke. When he heard this he feared for his wife and, rising early in the morning, ordered his servants to harness his horses. And without taking leave of the King, the Duke rode away with his Duchess, his knights, and all his company. Aww

When the King was told that he had departed, he grew very angry. He sent after the Duke, ordering him to return at once or else peace would terminate between them. But the Duke mocked him and returned to his country. There he fortified his entire land and strengthened all his cities and towers, for he knew that the king would wage war against him.

About three months thereafter the King summoned all his troops to attack the Duke. He marched and besieged the castle[24] wherein the Duke had sought protection. The Duchess was in another lofty castle,[25] and with her were her daughters, maids and valiant knights. But the King intensified the siege against the castle where the Duke had taken refuge and attacked it for many days in vain.

He then called Merlin and said to him:

---

[22] Cf. Esther 2:18, "Then the king made a great feast for all his princes and his servants," The Christmas feast of the Old French original (Cf. Sommer, II, p. 58) is changed by means of the biblical language of the popular Esther story into a Jewish feast.
[23] Cf. II Samuel 13:2, "Amnon became ill out of love for his sister, Tamar."
[24] Lit., "a fortified city." Cf. Isaiah 25:2, "For thou hast made of a fortified city a ruin."
[25] Lit, "a lofty city." Cf. Isaiah 26:5, "For he bringeth down them that dwell on high, the lofty city he layeth it low." The scribe has utilized two words in succeeding chapters of Isaiah to describe the medieval castle, which had no equivalent in biblical Hebrew.

17

עזריני בחכמתך אך הפעם* ותן עצה איך אוכל להיועד עם הדוכסית איזרנא
כי אנכי מת על חשקה אם לא תהי לי. ויאמר מרלין אני אעשה כך שאתן
לך צורת פני הדוכוס ותבנית כל גופו בעניין שהדוכסית תחשוב שאתה הוא
הדוכוס בעלה.

ואני אבוא עמך ואתן אלי צורת פל|וני| הפרש חבירו ובכן נרכוב בלילה
שנינו ונקרא אל שער הקריה אשר שם הדוכסית ויפתחו לנו ונבוא בהיכל
ואתה תיכנס בחדר ותשתעשע עמה כרצונך ואחר כן תקום ונצא ונשוב אל
החיל. וישתחו לו המלך. וכן עשה מרלין בחכמתו ויבא אליה ותהר לו.
ויקם מן המטה וירכבו שניהם ויצאו מן הקריה.

ובצאתם והנה בא רץ אחד אל הדוכסית לאמר איך נהרג הדוכוס בעלה
במלחמה בלילה ההוא. וכן היה האמת כי הדוכוס שמע שהמלך אוטיר
פנדרגון מת בתוך החיל ובכן יצא חוץ מן הקריה להלחם בחיל באותו הלילה
לרוע מזלו ונהרג במלחמה. ובשוב המלך אל החיל מצא הדוכוס מת מושכב
והקריה נלכדה וישמח.

והדוכסית נתאבלה על בעלה והיה לבה יוצא מן הפלא הגדול [75b]
ואומרת איך אפשר זה והלא הדוכס היה עמי במטה באותה שעה שאומרין
שנהרג שם בחיל כי הרץ בא אלי אל החדר ובצאתו מן הקריה לא הרחיק
/עד/יין כמטחוי קשת[ב] אם כן איך אפשר שנהרג שם, ואם נהרג אם כן אותו
שבא אלי לא היה הדוכוס.

א׳ שופטים טז,כח: ויקרא שמשון אל ה׳ ויאמר ... זכרני נא וחזקני נא אך הפעם
הזה.
ב׳ בראשית כא,טז: ותלך ותשב לה מנגד הרחק כמטחוי קשת.

18

"Oh brother, pray help me only this time[26] with your art, and advise me how I can meet the Duchess Izerna, for I shall certainly die of desire if she be not mine."

"What I shall do," said Merlin, "is to endow you with the Duke's likeness and appearance so that the Duchess will think that you are the Duke, her husband. And I shall come with you in the guise of a certain knight, his companion. Thus both of us shall ride at night and call to the Duchess' gatekeeper. He will admit us and we shall enter the castle. You will enter her chamber and take your delight with her as you desire. Then you will rise and we shall leave and return to our army."

The King listened to him. And Merlin accomplished this through his art. And he [Uter Pendragon] came to her and she conceived. Then he rose from the bed and the two of them rode out of the castle.

As they departed, a messenger came to the Duchess informing her that her husband had been slain that very night. Indeed it was true. The Duke had heard that King Uter Pendragon had been killed in battle, so he left his castle that night to contend with the foe but, to his ill luck, was killed in battle. When the King returned to his camp, he rejoiced to find the Duke lying dead and the castle taken by his army.

The Duchess mourned her husband and grew faint-hearted at the wondrous event.

"How is it possible?" she said. "Wasn't the Duke in bed with me at that very hour when they say he was killed in battle? No sooner had he gone more than a bow-shot's distance away[27] from the castle than the messenger came straight to my chamber. So how is it possible that he was killed there? And if indeed he was killed, the one who came to me was not the Duke."

[26] Cf. Judges 16:28, "And Samson called unto the Lord and said, 'pray strengthen me only this time.'" Here again, a paraphrase of an extremely popular biblical verse lends Hebraic tonal color to the story.
[27] Cf. Genesis 21:16, "She [Hagar] went and sat down a bowshot's distance away..." (My translation, based on the new translation of the Torah, Philadelphia, 1962.)

19

בזו המחשבה היתה משתו/מ/מת ובוכה ולא היתה יכולה להשיג אמיתת זה
העניין.   אז נפרד המלך מן הקריה ויבוא אל קרית הדוכסית ויצר עליה,
סוף דבר הוצרכה לתת לו הקריה.   והיו מליצים רבים בינו לבינה והדברים
ארוכים.   באחרית ניתנה העצה שהמלך אוטיר פנדרגון לכבודו ולמען הפיס
רצון הדוכסית ורצון שרי הדוכוס ורצון כל עם ארצו ישא את הדוכסית
לאשה. וישיא את ד' בנותיה לד' מלכים או רוזנים.

וכשמוע המלך את העצה הזו שניתנה מאת שריו וחכמיו שמח עד מאד וכן
עשה.   את הדוכסית נשא הוא ואחת מבנותיה הגדולה השיא אל המלך לוט
מאורקניאה והיו לו ממנה ד' בנים שם האחד הגדול היה מסיר גלוין, והשני
גדריאט, השלישי אגרבן, הרביעי גווידן, השנית השיא אל המלך אוריאנש
והוליד ממנה מסיר איבן.   השלישית השיא אל הדוכוס מקיירנצוא. הרביעית
לא רצתה לינשא לאיש אבל למדה חכמת השדים והיא היתה מורגאא.

ויהי בלילה אחד והמלך היה משתעשע עם הדוכסית במטה ונתן יד על
כריסה ויאמר לה הנה את הרה הידעת ממי את הרה.   השיבה לא ידעתי
כי מן הדוכוס לא הריתי הפעם כי בהשתגבו בקריה לא הניחני הרה.   ובלילה
שבא אלי איש אחד בצורתו ותבניתו לא ידעתי מי היה כי בוודאי לא היה
הדוכוס.   כי בשעה שאותו הפרש היה עמי במטה אז נהרג הדוכוס בחיל.
ולכן איני יודעת מה היה לי וממי אנכי הרה.   והמלך עצר בעצמו ולא
רצה להגיד אליה שהוא היה הבא אליה ויאמר אליה הואיל שאין את יודעת
ממי את הרה כשתלדי ינתן הילד אל מרלין שהוא יודע בחכמת השדים ויקרא

20

Thinking thus, she would wonder and cry, but could not get to the heart of the matter.

Then the King departed from the castle and came to the castle of the Duchess. After his siege she finally had to surrender it to him. There were many discussions between them, (but these matters are lengthy.[28]) *LOL*

Finally a suggestion was offered that the King – for his own honor and in order to pacify the Duchess, the Duke's officers and all the people of the land – marry the Duchess and marry her four daughters to four kings or princes.

When the King heard the suggestion offered by his officers and councilors, he joyfully acquiesced. He married the Duchess; and her eldest daughter he married to King Lot of Orcania. From her he had four sons: Sir Galwan, the eldest; the second, Gadriat;[29] the third, Agravan; the fourth, Gwidon. The second daughter he married to King Uriens; he begat Sir Ivan. The third daughter he married to the Duke of Kairenza. The fourth daughter did not wish to marry, but learned the art of witchcraft – her name was Morgana. *Hell Yea!*

One night as the King was taking his delight in bed with the Duchess, he placed his hand on her belly and said:

"You are with child. Do you know who the father is?"

"I do not know," she replied. "I certainly did not conceive this time by the Duke, for when he retreated to his castle he did not leave me with child. That night someone who bore his shape and likeness came to me. I do not know who he was; it certainly was not the Duke, for just when that knight was in bed with me the Duke was killed in battle. Therefore, I do not know what happened to me and by whom I have conceived."

But the King restrained himself and did not wish to tell her that it was he who had come to her. *He's a liar*

"Since you do not know who fathered the child," he said, "when you give birth the child will be given to Merlin, who knows the art

---

[28] The same phrase that the scribe has used previously to indicate a point of abridgement. See Chap. 4 for further discussion.
[29] I.e., Gaharias.

שמו ארטושין כלומ|ו|ר| שנולד בכח ארטי.

וזה אמר המלך בעבור כי מרלין השביעו כשהביאו אל חדר הדוכסית שאם
היא תתעבר מאותה ביאה שיתן לו את הילד היולד שיהיה שלו ויעשה ממנו
כרצונו וכן נשבע לו וכן קיים לו כאשר תראה קרוב לסוף הספר. ובכן
נולד ממנה ארטושין הוא היה המלך הגדול שנקרא ארטוש. נמצא אם כן שכל
אותם ד' הפרשים האחים הנזכרים לעיל שהיו בני הבת הגדולה של הדוכסית
איזרנא מן המלך לוט היו נכדים שלהמלך ארטוש מצד האם כלומר בני
אחותו מצד האם.   גם מסיר איבן היה נכדו בזה הענין.   ומרורגנא היתה אחותו
מצד האם.
אבל מורדריט הרשע המסור עמד בחזקת נכדו שנים רבות וכן היה המלך
עצמו אומר עליו, אמנם באחרית נודע שהיה בנו ממזר כאשר תראה כתוב
בספר השמד.

ויהי כאשר שב בורז אל החצר בעיר קמלוט מארץ רחוקה כמו מירושלים
נתקבל בחצר המלך בכבוד גדול ובצהלה רבה.   וכאשר סיפר פטירת גלאץ
ומיתת פרנציבל נתעצבו מאד כל בני החצר.

22

of sorcery. He will be called *Artusin*, that is, born through the power of *art*.[30]

Man has power over woman if pregnant many

The King said this because when Merlin brought him to the Duchess' chamber he had made the King swear that if she would conceive from that coition he would give Merlin the child to do with as he pleased. The King swore and kept his oath, as you will see near the end of the book. And so she gave birth to Artusin, who is the great king called Artus.

King Artus

We see then that all four knights, the brothers mentioned above, the children of the Duchess Izerna's eldest daughter and of King Lot, were nephews of King Artus on his mother's side. Similarly, Sir Ivan was his nephew; Morgana was his sister on his mother's side. But the evil traitor Mordred passed himself off as a nephew for many years. Even the King conceded this. However, finally it became known that he was a bastard son, as you will see in the book of destruction.

When Borz returned to the court in the city of Camelot from a land as distant as Jerusalem, he was received at the King's court with great honor and much tumult. And when he told of the passing of Galaç[31] and the death of Prenzival,[32] everyone in the court was deeply grieved. Then King Artus ordered that all the

---

[30] Naming a child after an event is traditional in the Bible. Beginning with Adam and continuing through all the heroes, there is either a sound philological basis or folk-etymology operating with all the names. For instance, Rachel called her first son Joseph (Yosef) because "The Lord add (yosef) to me another son." Genesis 30:24. Also, Moses' mother "called his name Moses (moshe) because I drew him (masha) from the water". Exodus 2:10. In the Arthurian legends, Tristan gets his name because of the sadness of his mother, who dies at childbirth. Cf. the Rachel-Benjamin story (Genesis 35: 16-19). The naming of Artusin, above, is most likely an addition of the Hebrew scribe. Such a pattern of naming does not appear in the O.F.

[31] Italian forms for Galehut are "Galeotto, Galas, Galeas, Galeasso..." See Gardner, p. 120.

[32] No variation akin to this is cited in Fernand Flutre's *Table des noms propres avec toutes leurs variants figurant dans romans du moyen age ecrits en francais ou en provencal et actuellement publies ou analyses*, Poitiers, 1962. Future references to this work will be abbreviated to Flutre. However, a thirteenth century Italian sonnet by Guitone contains the line: "si come Prenzevallo a non cherere..." See Gardner, pp. 29-30.

23

אז צוה המלך ארטוש שכל הקורות אשר חלו על הפרשים שהלכו אל חיפוש התמחוי[א] יכתבו וישומו בספר למזכרת ויעש. ואותו הוא הסיפור שלהספר התמחוי הנקרא[א] ליברו דילא קשטא דיל סנגראאל.

אחר זה אמר[ו] המלך אל פקידיו תנו לב לדעת כמה נפקדו מפרשי הטבלא בזה החיפוש. וימצאו שנפקדו[ב] מהם מ"ב שמתו במלחמת החיפוש בגבורת כלי זיין ופרשות. וישבע המלך ארטוש את מסיר גלוון נכדו שיאמר אליו באמת כמה הרג מהם בחרבו.

ויאמר מסיר גלוון בשבועתו כי הרג מהם בידו י"ח פרשים טובים. וישאלהו המלך אם היה בכלל הי"ח מלך בנו ממאגוץ. ויאמר כן היה ועליו דוה[ג] לבי וידווה כל הימים אמנם לא הכרתיו במלחמה. ענה המלך וכן אנכי דוה ונעצב עליו עד מאד כי היה חבירי ואוהבי נאמני.

וכאשר ידע המלך כמה חסרו מפרשי הטבלא במלחמת התמחוי ציוה לבחור אחרים תחתיהם כמספרם כדי להשלים מספר הטבלא. ויבחרו מ"ב

א· פאה ח,ז: מי שיש לא מזון שתי סעודות לא יטל מן התמחוי.
ב· השווה שמואל-ב ב,ל: ויפקדו מעבדי דוד תשעה עשר איש ועשהאל.
ג· השווה איכה ה,יז: על זה היה דוה לבנו.

events which befell the knights who went on the Quest of the Dish[33] should be recorded in a memorial volume. And so it was done. And that is the story of the Book of the Dish which is called *Libro di la Kesta del Sangraal.*

After this the King said to his officers: "Mark how many knights of the Table are missing from this Quest."

They found that forty-two were missing,[34] having died in the war of the Quest through valor of arms and knighthood. King Artus commanded his nephew Sir Galwan upon his oath to tell him truthfully how many of them he killed with his sword.

Sir Galwan said upon oath that he personally had killed eighteen good knights.

The King asked him if Bano of Magoç[35] was included among these eighteen.

"Yes," he replied, "and my heart grieves[36] for him and will grieve forever, for I did not recognize him in battle."

The King replied, "I too am very grieved and saddened over him, for he was my loving and loyal friend."

When the King learned how many of the knights of the Table were lost in the war of the Dish, he ordered a like number to be chosen in their stead to complete the number at the Table. They

---

[33] Obviously the grail. But the word that the scribe chose – *tamchuy* – would give the Hebrew reader an entirely different meaning. *Tamchuy* is a charity bowl, from which food was distributed to the hungry and the needy. See Mishna Peah 8:7 and Chapter 4. According to Chretien, the grail was a platter, large and deep enough to hold a pike, a lamprey, or a salmon. (See R. S. Loomis, *The Grail: From Celtic Myth to Christian Symbol*, N. Y. 1963, p. 29.) Coincidentally, the *tamchuy* too seemed to be a platter. As far as can be discerned from another citation (Mishna Kelim 16:1), the *tamchuy* was a "dish made with several partitions for food." I am quite sure that the Hebrew scribe chose the word *tamchuy* not because of its resemblance to Chretien's *graal*, but on the contrary, because of its deep Jewish significance. For *tamchuy* see also Y. Brand, *Kley ha-Kheres B'Sifrut ha-Talmud*, Jerusalem, 1953, Chap. 125, p. 539.

[34] Cf. II Samuel 2:30, "...and when he had gathered all the people together nineteen of David's servants were missing and Ashael."

[35] I.e., Bagdemagus. Another form of this name in Italian is Bando di Mago (Gardner, p. 338).

[36] Cf. Lamentations 5:17, "Our heart grieves for this."

פרשים טובים וגיבורים אמנם היו בחורים לא ניסו עצמם עדיין היטב ולא
למדו דרכי מלחמת שדה כמספיקא. ויצו לעשות סיבוב אחד באחו שלעיר
וינצשטרי ליום נועד למען למד דרכי מלחמה וגבורות פרשות אל אלו
הפרשים החדשים ויקרב יום המלחמה.

ועתה נתחיל לדבר מאודות הפרש הנעלה מסיר לנצולוט דללק בן מלך בנו
דבנואוק. יש לדעת כי כאשר הלכו הפרשים שלהטבלא אל מלחמת חיפוש
התמחוי ומסיר לנץ בראשם טרם לכתו במלחמה הלך אל גלח אחד עצור
בעצרה אחת שהיה המוודה שלו. ויתודה ממנו על חטאותיו וגם על מה שהיה
נואף אל המלכה זנברא. וילך אל החיפוש.

ובשובו מן החיפוש הלך עוד אל המוודה להוודות על חטא הרציחות אשר
עשה במלחמת החיפוש. ויצוהו המוודה לעשות תשובה בצום ובתחינות כך
וכך ימים. ובכן נעצר שם עמו ימים רבים לעשות את תשובתו. ואיש לא
ידע בימים ההם אנא פנה כי נסתרה דרכו מכל חביריו ופרשי החצר ושנייו
בורז וליאונל אשטור והמלך היו משתוממים עד מאד מפרידתו.

ויהי כאשר תמו ימי תשובתו והוא יצא מן העצרה וילחץ וירכב על סוסו ובא
לחצר המלך. וכאשר הגיע אל החצר היה היום יום בשורה אל המלך וכל
הפרשים וכל בני החצר. וכל אנשי עיר קמלוט צהלו ושמחו ויעשו יום טוב
גדול. אמנם המלכה זנברא אשת המלך שמחה בביאתו יותר מכולם אלף
פעם כי כל ימי העלמו בעצרה היו ימיה ימי אבל ובכי בסתר והתחלתה.

chose forty-two good and valorous knights; however, they were youths who had not adequately proved themselves and had not sufficiently learned the art of war in the field.

He ordered a tournament to be held on a certain day in the field of Wincestre so as to teach the new knights the art of warfare and knightly valor.

The day of battle approached.

Now let us begin to speak of that exalted knight, Sir Lancelot del Lac, son of King Bano de Benoic. It is necessary to know that when the knights of the Table departed for the battle in Quest of the Dish, Lanç led them. Before leaving for battle he went to his confessor, a monk who had shut himself into a retreat, and he confessed all his sins to him, including that of adultery with Queen Zinevra.[37] He then went on the Quest and, upon his return from the Quest, went once more to the confessor to confess the murders he had committed during the battle of the Quest. The confessor ordered him to repent by fasting and supplication for a certain length of time. He remained there with him for many days to enact his repentance.

During those days no one knew where he was, for he had concealed his whereabouts from all his friends. The knights of the court, his cousins Borz and Lionel, his brother Estor, and the King were all very astounded by his disappearance. Once the days of his repentance were completed, he left the retreat, mounted, and rode his horse to the King's court. When he reached the court it was a day of glad tidings for the King, and all the knights and members of the court. Everyone in the city of Camelot merrily rejoiced and made it a festive day of celebration.

But at his arrival[38] the joy of Queen Zinevra, the King's wife, was a thousand-fold greater than all the others. For all the days of his seclusion at the retreat were days of mourning, secret weeping and indisposition. No wonder, for strong as death is the love[39]

---

[37] An Italian sonnet by Florentine Maestro in the second half of the thirteenth century makes mention of "Ginevra", referring to King Arthur's wife. See Gardner, p. 34.

[38] There is a double entendre in Hebrew. *Bi'ah* can also mean the sexual act. See B. T. Yoma 86 b, and Mishna Kedushin 1:1.

[39] Cf. Song of Songs 8:6, "For strong as death is love."

ואין לתמיה בזה כי עזה^א כמות האהבה אשר אהבתהו מן היום אשר התייחדה עמו בפיתויי מסיר גאלוט כאשר יאמר סיפור אחר. ומסיר לנץ גם הוא החל לשוב אל חשקו ולחשוק בה כמלפנים ויותר אלף פעמים. ואם מאז היה חושק בחכמה ומכסה פשעיו עתה החל לפרסם את חשקו יותר מידאי בעניין רע.

והיא גם כן מצידה עד שכל בני החצר בכלל ואגרבן בפרט היו מרגישים בדבר כשהיא היתה מהדרת ומקשטת עצמה בכל עוז מרוב חיבתו עד שהיתה מסכנת כל רואיה מרוב הפלגת יופיה. והתחיל העם להרנין על שניהם לאמר כי היו נאחזים לז בלו בחבלי אהבה עזה וחשק סכלי. וזה החשק הרע היה סיבת השמד הטבלא ומיתת מלך ארטוש ואבדן כל המלכות כאשר תראה לפנים.

ויהי כאשר [76a] אגרבן אח מסיר גלוון הרגיש בדבר שמח מאד כי היה אויב אל מסיר לנץ ויאמר בלבו עתה מצאתי הנקודה להנקם מלנץ אז נאספו פרשים רבים מכל צד אל החצר כדי ללכת אל הסיבוב שלוויינצשטרי ולנץ היה מעלים מאד את הליכתו שם בעבור שלא היה רוצה שהפרשים האכסנאים אשר באו אל הסיבוב ימנעו מהיכנס במערכה מפחדתם פן יפגע גם הוא מחמת היותם יראים מהפלגת גבורתו ועוד כדי שיוכל להיות מאי זה צד שירצה.

ולכן הסתיר מכל איש את הליכתו ועשה את עצמו חולה בדבריו ואמר| אל כל חביריו שלא היה בו כח לבוא אל הסיבוב. אמנם ציוה את בורז וליאונל שנייו ואת אשטור אחיו שילכו הם אל הסיבוב עם כל חברתו והם ממאנים ללכת בלעדיו, סוף דבר הפציר בם וציום שילכו עם המלך וכן עשו.

ויהי כראות אגרבן את בורז וליאונל ואשטור וכל חברת לנץ מכינים עצמם ללכת והוא נשאר לאלתר חשב בלבו להלשין את לנץ אל המלך (אל המלך)

א. שיר השירים ח,ו: כי עזה כמות אהבה.

which she had for him from the day she was united with him, enticed by Sir Galot, as is seen in another tale.[40]

Once again Sir Lanç' passion returned, and he desired her a thousand-fold more than before. And whereas he would previously desire her discreetly and cover up his sins, he now exceeded the mark in displaying his desire in this evil matter, and she likewise, until the entire court in general and Agravan in particular perceived this. She beautified and adorned herself with all her might out of the great love she had for him, so that she endangered all who beheld her with the excessive display of her beauty. Then the people began to murmur about the two of them, saying that both were caught in the bonds of strong love and foolish passion. And this evil desire was the cause of the destruction of the Table, the death of King Artus, and the ruin of the entire Kingdom,[41] as you will see further on.

When Agravan, the brother of Sir Galwan, noticed this, he rejoiced greatly because he was a foe to Sir Lanç. He said in his heart, "Now I have found occasion wherewith I can take revenge upon Lanç." Many knights then came from all sides and gathered in the court in order to go to the tournament at Wincestre. But Lanç concealed his participation, because he did not want fear to prevent the new knights who had come to the tournament from entering the contest, lest he too lose glory by their dreading the display of his strength. Moreover, he wanted to be able to support whichever side he chose.

Therefore he concealed his going from everyone, feigned illness, and told his friends that he had no strength to go to the tournament. However, he ordered his cousins Borz and Lionel and his brother Estor to proceed to the tournament with his company. But they refused to go without him. Finally he urged them to leave, ordering them to go with the King, which they did. When Agravan saw that Borz, Lionel and Estor, and all of Lanç' company preparing to depart while he remained behind, he thought of denouncing Lanç

---

[40] See Sommer, III, 253 ff.

[41] For the Hebrew reader sin as cause of destruction is a familiar biblical theme. See Deut. 28:15-68, the Book of Amos, and other prophets.

דודו ולגלות לו כל העניין מן המלכה. ויבוא אל המלך דודו ויאמר לו דבר
סתר גדול ארצה לאמר לך לכבודך ולטובתך ולהסיר את כלימתך אם הייתי
רשאי לאומרו. אמ|ר| המלך היש בחצר איש גדול כל כך שיהיה רשאי
לחשוב את כלמתי.

ענה אגרבן יש ויש. כי המלכה ולנצולוט חושקים לז בלז מחשק הסכלי עד
מאד ולבעבור שלנץ אינו יכול להשתעשע עמה להנאתו בעודך בהיכל הוא
מחלה עצמו בדבריו ונמנע מלכת אל הסיבוב ושולח שם את כל חברייו ואחרי
נוסעך יתייחד עם המלכה יעלוס עמה להנאתו כרצונו. כשמוע המלך כן הפליג
לדבריו ולא יכול להאמינו. ויאמר לו נכדי אל תוסף דבר אלי עוד
(ה)/ב/דבר הזה כי איני מאמינך למען אשר ידעתיו לי לאוהב נאמן.
ואי אפשר שחשב לעשות מסירות כזה בשום עניין. ואם חשב אונס חשק
הכריחו לעשות כן כי נגד מחשבת חשק לא יוכל עמוד לא דת ולא שכל.
כו|ל| ש|כן| חשק זנברא שיופיה הוא מופלא כל כך שאפי|לו| הקדושים יתמהו
עליו וישתוקקו לראותו. אמנם חלילה לי מהאמין שהיה מביא מחשבתו לפועל.
אמר אגרבן דודי אם כן אני רו(צ)/א/ה שאין רצונך לעשות על זה דבר
ולחשוב שום עניין אחר על לנץ.

אמ|ר| המלך ומה תרצה שאעשה. ענה אגרבן ארצה שתשתדל אהת ואני בכל
עניין שנוכל שנמצאם יחד בייחוד מגונה ואז תדע האמת ותאמין לדבריי פעם
אחרת. אמ|ר| המלך מזה עשה כרצונך כי אני מסכים לכך אבל ידעתי כי

before the King and revealing the entire affair concerning the Queen.

He came to the King his uncle and said to him:

"With your permission to speak, I have an important secret that I want to tell you concerning your honor and welfare, and the removal of your shame."

The King said, "Is there a man so great in the court who can think about shaming me?"

"Certainly there is," replied Agravan, "for the Queen and Lancelot desire each other with a most foolish passion. And since Lancelot cannot take his delight with her to his heart's content while you are still in the palace, he claims to be ill and unable to go to the tournament and sends his entire company there. After your departure he will unite with the Queen and will enjoy her according to his pleasure and will."

When the King heard this, he thought it an exaggeration and could not believe it. He said to him: "Nephew, nephew, speak no more to me of this matter, for I do not believe you. I know him to be loyal and loving. And it is impossible that he thought of doing such an act of treachery under any circumstances. Even if he intended to, it was the force of his desire which compelled him to do this, for neither law nor reason can withstand thoughts of desire. This is certainly true concerning desire for Zinevra, whose beauty is so marvelous that even the saints[42] are amazed at it and yearn to see it. But I cannot believe that he would carry out his thoughts."

"Uncle, if such is the case," said Agravan, "then I see[43] that you don't intend to do anything about this matter, nor think any more about Lanç."

"What do you want me to do?" said the King.

"I would like us to try to discover them both in despicable union, and then you will know the truth and believe me at some other time."

"Then do as you like," said the King, "for I agree to it. But I know that he will never be thus discovered."

---

[42] The Hebrew has no equivalent for *saint*, but approximates it via the word *k'doshim* (*the holy ones*), a term filled with Jewish associations.
[43] Lit. "want" (rozeh), whereas the context calls for "see" (ro'eh). A curve to a ligature changed one word to another.

31

לעולם לא ימצא. ענה אגרבן דיי לי במה שאמרת עתה. וכל הלילה היה
המלך חושב ומשתאה על דברי אגרבן האפשר כן אם לא. ותמיד היה מתחזק
על האי אפשר מטוב בטחונו באהבת לנץ באמונתו.

לבוקר הכין המלך את כל פרשיו לנסוע ללכת אל הסיבוב שלווינצשטרי
והמלכה חלתה פניו מאד שיביאה עמו אל הסיבוב מתאוותה לראות הקיבוץ
הגדול מן הפרשות שיתקבץ שם ולא שמע אליה המלך למען נסות את דברי
אגרבן. ויסע המלך ופרשיו ומדי רוכבם היו מדברים ביניהם רק מאודות
לנץ ודואגים על חוליו שמנעהו מבוא אל הסיבוב.

ותכף צאתם מן העיר קם לנץ ממטתו והכין עצמו ללכת שפי אל הסיבוב
בעניין שלא ינכר שם. ויבוא אל המלכה ויאמר לה גבירתי הנעימה אם טוב
בעיניך יש ברצוני ללכת אל הסיבוב ברשותך. ותען המלכה חביבי מדוע
איחרת ומה היה לך שלא הלכת עם המלך.

אמר לנץ איחרתי כי אין רצוני שיכירני אדם לא בלכתי ולא בהיותי שם כי
בהיותי בסיבוב אעזור אל אי זו כת שיראה לי לכבוד ולגבורה יותר. אמרה
המלכה חביבי נעימי לך לשלום ולשמחה עם אהבתי וחשקי ועשה חיל וגבורות
כמנהגך הטוב. ויען לנץ ומי הוא הפרש ואפי|לו| אם יהי לו לבב שפן
שלא יתחדש לו לבב הארי בגבורה ובעוז אם יהיה מוכתר מאהבת גבירה
כמוני היום המאושר על כל המאושרים חן לש|ם| ואליך.

וישקה ויחבקה וישתעשעו יחד באהבים בשעה אחת. וירכב ויסע הוא ונושא
כליו שניהם לבדם בבוקר בטרם יכיר איש את רעהו ויהיו משמאילים מן
המסילה כל היום ההוא למען לא יפגשו במי שיכירהו. ולבקר טרם יום הגיע

"What you have just said suffices for me," replied Agravan.

Throughout the night the King thought and wondered whether Agravan's words were true or not, yet he tended to disbelieve them out of his genuine confidence in Lanç' love and loyalty.

The next morning the King prepared all his knights for the trip to the tournament at Wincestre. The Queen implored him to take her with him to the tournament, for she yearned to see the great gathering of knighthood that would assemble there. But in order to put Agravan's words to the test, the King did not heed her.

While the King and his knights rode they spoke only of Lanç, expressing their concern about the illness which prevented him from coming to the tournament.

As soon as the knights left the city Lanç arose from his bed and prepared himself to go alone to the tournament, so that he would not be recognized there. He came to the Queen and said to her:

"My dear lady, if it pleases you, I request your permission to go to the tournament."

"My beloved," said the Queen, "why did you tarry? Why did you not go with the King?"

"I tarried," said Lanç, "because I did not wish to be recognized by anyone, neither during my journey nor during my stay there, for once at the tournament I shall help the side from which I can achieve greater honor and valor."

"My dear love," said the Queen, "go in peace and joy with my loving desire, and be victorious and valorous as is your wont."

"Even a rabbit-hearted knight," answered Lanç, "would become lion-hearted, brave and valorous, were he crowned with the love of his lady as I, happiest of men, am today, thanks to God[44] and to you."

Whereupon he kissed her and embraced her and they engaged in love-play for an hour.

Then at dawn, when recognition is impossible, he and his armor-bearer rode off unobserved. All day long they strayed from the beaten track in order not to meet anyone who might recognize them. Before daybreak Lanç reached the town where the King had en-

[44] The Hebrew has only the first letter (h) of the word *ha-shem*, "the Name". (See note 10, p. 13). Lanç, then, is utilizing the pious Jew's mode of referring to God.

33

בכרך אחד שהמלך חנה שם והתכוון להיכנס שם בבוקר כדי שלא יכירהו
שום אחד מפרשי המלך. ושם זה הכרך אשקאלוט שלקצין אחד ושמו לנבל
בבאסור דאשקאלוט.

ובעלות השחר והמלך השכים למען הכין עצמו אל הרכיבה והיה עומד בחלון
ההיכל שחנה בו וישקף וראה את סוס לנץ ויכירהו כי הוא נתנו אליו במתנה
אמנם את לנץ לא הכיר אז כי היה מעולף וכסוי פנים מאד באלמו וזיניו.
אבל מדי עוברו ממבוי אל מבוי לא נזהר לנץ מן המלך ונשא את ראשו ובכן
הורם את אלמו מעט מעל פניו וראהו המלך והכירו.

ויראהו אל גופלט ויאמר לו בחשאי הראית את לנץ אשר תמול היה מח/לה
עצמו בדבריו למראה עינים והנה הנו בכרך הזה. ענה גופלט אני חושב
שעשה כן כדי להסתיר עצמו בל יכירהו כי כן מנהגו. אמ|ר| המלך וכן
האמת. ארורים יהיו כל הרכילים ומוצאי דיבה על הפרשים הנאמנים ולנץ
לא ידע שהוכר מעיני המלך וילך ויחן בהיכל הקצין.
ויתקבל שם בכבוד גדול כחוק הקצין לכבד כל פרש ולא מחמת שהכירו.
והמלך ציוה את גופלט בל יגלה לאיש שבא לנץ אל הסיבוב אחרי שהוא
רוצה להכסות פן יחר לו. ועתה מניח הספר מדבר מן המלך ושב לדבר
רק מלנץ ומן קצין אשקאלוט ובניו ובתולתו.

יש לדעת כי קצין אשקאלוט היו לו ב' בנים גיבורים שנתפרשו מיד המלך
מזמן קרוב.

camped. He intended to enter in the morning so that none of the King's knights would recognize him. The name of this town was Askalot, and it belonged to a lord called Lanval,[45] vavasour of Askalot.

At dawn the King rose to prepare himself for the journey and stood at the window of the castle where he had lodged. He looked out and saw Lanç' horse; he recognized it because he had given it to him as a present. But he did not recognize Lanç for his face was well-covered with his helmet and his armor. But in passing from one path to another, Lanç, unaware of the King, raised his head, thereby slightly lifting his helmet from his face. The King saw him and recognized him. He pointed Lanç out to Goflet and softly said to him:

"Do you see Lanç who yesterday, to all appearance, claimed to be ill, and yet is here in town now?"

"I think he did this," Goflet replied, "in order to be able to conceal himself and prevent recognition, for such is his custom."

"That's the truth," said the King, "and cursed be all who bear tales and slander loyal knights."

Lanç did not know that he was recognized by the King. He went on and lodged in the castle of the lord, where he was received with great honor, not because he knew him, but because it was the lord's custom to honor every knight.

The King ordered Goflet not to reveal to any one that Lanç had come to the tournament, lest he be angry, since it was his wish to remain incognito.

Now the book leaves the King and speaks once more only of Lanç and the lord of Askalot, his sons and his daughter.

Know that the lord of Askalot had two valiant sons who had recently been knighted[46] by the King. The older one was called

---

[45] The *Mort Artu* gives no name to the lord of Askalot; neither does it identify his two sons, who are later named in the Hebrew ms. See Chapter 6.
[46] The scribe had to coin this term, for Hebrew had no working vocabulary for the knightly world. Staying within the pliable root-structure of Hebrew, he took the biblical noun for horseman (P-R-Sh), cast it into the reflexive aspect and coined the verb *to be knighted*, or *to become a knight*. This is the first time to my knowledge that this verb appears in Hebrew literature.

שם הגדול אדלפרט ושם הקטן קרבוץ ולהם זינים אדומים כולם מצבע אחד
אדום כי כן מנהג המתפרשים שלא ישאו זיין בשנה ראשונה שהתפרשו אלא
מצבע אחד ונקרא הפרש כל אותה שנה הפרש החדש. וישא לנץ את עיניו
וירא את מגיניהם וזיניהם כולם אדומים. אמ]ור[לנץ אל הבלבסור אדוני אני
מחלה פניך שתשאילני זוג אחד מאלה שני הזינים ומגן אחד לשאת בזה הקיבוץ
וכן כלי מכסה הסוס.

ענה הבאבסור האין אתך מגן.   אמ]ור[לנץ אין לי מגן שארצה לשאת בסיבוב
הזה כי אין רצוני להנכר בזה הקיבוץ.   אבל אם יישר בעיניך אקח את אלה
הזינים ואת זיניי ומגיני אניח הנה עד שובי.   ענה הקצין קח לך את זיני קרבוץ
שהוא חולה ולא יוכל לבוא אל הסיבוב ואדלפרט אחיו הגדול יבוא עמך
אל הסיבוב ותתחברו יחדיו.

וישמח לנץ בדברי הקצין ויחננהו מאד ויאמר מה נעמה לי חברת
אדלפרט [76] ומה שפרה עלי.   ויסכימו שניהם ללכת יחדיו.   וישאל אדלפרט
את לנץ מה שמך אדוני ויאמר לנץ אנכי פרש אחד נע בא ממלכות לוגריש
ללכת אל הסיבוב ווינצשטרי ואת שמו לא הגיד לו[א].   ולנץ עמד שם כל
היום ההוא להכין עצמו היטב מכל דבר הראוי לפרש.

א. שופטים יג,ז: ואת שמו לא הגיד לי.

36

Edelpert[47] and the younger one Karavoç.[48] They had armor wholly of one color, red, for such was the custom of new knights – to wear armor only of one color during their first year. Throughout the year the knight would be called a new knight.

Lanç looked up at their shields and armor and saw that they were entirely red. He said to the valvasour[49]:

"My lord, I implore you to lend me one of these two suits of armor and one shield to carry at the gathering, and also a covering for my horse."

"Haven't you a shield?" answered the vavasour.

"I don't have a shield that I would want to carry in this tournament, because I do not wish to be recognized there. But if you agree I shall take this armor, and leave my armor and shield here until I return."

"Take Karavoç's armor," said the lord. "He is ill and cannot go to the tournament. His older brother Edelpert will accompany you to the tournament and you will be companions."

Lanç rejoiced at the lord's words and was very pleased with him. He said:

"How pleasant, how delightful Edelpert's company will be!"

So they both agreed to go together.

"What is your name, sir?" Edelpert asked Lanç.

"I am a knight-errant from the Kingdom of Logris on my way to the tournament at Wincestre."

But he did not tell him his name.[50]

Lanç remained there that day to provide himself thoroughly with everything necessary for a knight. The maiden daughter of the lord

---

[47] Since the Hebrew ms. has no vowels, only the letters A (or: E), D, L, P (or: F), R, and T appear in the text. No parallel to this name appears in Flutre, and so the correct reading of the name is therefore a matter of conjecture.

[48] This name, too, has no parallel in Flutre. It could be based on Caradoç, but he is not related to the lord of Askalot.

[49] The scribe spells this Italian word, transliterated in his Hebrew text, two different ways.

[50] Judges 13:7. Samson's mother, speaking about her encounter with the man of God, says: "But I did not ask him whence he was and he did not tell me his name."

והבתולה בת הקצין היתה יחידה ביופיה בכל אותה המלכות וחכמה ומשכלת. ותחמוד בלבבה[א] את יפי לנץ ותאלך[ב] את נושא כליו עד מאד כל היום ההוא שיודיענה מי הוא זה הפרש ומה שמו. ויאמר גברתי זהו הפרש המובחר שבעולם ואיני רשאי לומר לך עוד מאודותיו. אמרה ברוך תהיה דיי לי במה שאמרת ואיני צריכה לדעת עוד ממך.

לאלתר הרגישה מדברי נערו שהוא מסיר לנצולוט דללק /כ/(ב)שהוא היה נקרא בפי כל הפרש המובחר שבכל העולם ויבער חשקו בלבבה ולא יכלה להעלימו. ותבוא ותכרע לפני לנץ ואמרה. אדוני הפרש הנכבד אני שואלת ממך מתנה אחת התנגה אלי. לאלתר עמד לנץ ויושט[ג] את ידו ויקימיה ויאמר גברתי מאד חרה לי על אשר כרעת לפני. ומה שאלתך ותנתן לך[ד] אם אוכל.

אמרה תידור לי כן מצד האמונה שיש לך עם מי שאתה מחבב יותר. ענה כן אני נודר. אמרה לו אני שואלת ממך שתשא בסיבוב את זאת בית זרועי בפנון אחד על האלמו שלך בעבור אהבתי. כשמוע לנץ כבד עליו הדבר הזה עד מאד. אמנם מחמת ההשבעה שהשביעתו ואשר נדר לא היה רשאי למאן אבל דאג שקיבלה בשכבר נתן כל לבו וחשקו אל המלכה ופחד פן יוודע אליה הדבר בשום עת ויחר לה ותשנאנו.

א. הש׳ משלי ו,כה: אל תחמד יפיה בלבבך.
ב. הש׳ שופטים טז,טז: ויהי כי הציקה לו בדבריה כל הימים ותאלצהו.
ג. הש׳ מגלת אסתר ה,ב: ויושט המלך לאסתר את שרביט הזהב.
ד. מגלת אסתר ז,ב: ויאמר המלך לאסתר... מה שאלתך... ותנתן לך.

was the most beautiful in the kingdom, and intelligent and wise. In her heart she lusted after Lanç' beauty[51] and all that day strongly pressed[52] his armor-bearer to reveal the knight's identity and name.

"My lady," he said, "he is the most peerless knight in the world and I am forbidden to tell you any more about him."

"Blessed are you," she said. "What you have said satisfied me; I don't have to know any more from you."

She immediately guessed from the lad's words that he was Sir Lancelot del Lac, known among all the knights as the most peerless knight in the world. Her desire for him burned in her heart and she could not conceal it. She came and kneeled before Lanç and said:

"Honored Sir Knight, if I ask one gift of you, would you grant it to me?"

Lanç stood immediately, stretched out[53] his hand and raised her up.

"My lady, I deeply regret that you have kneeled before me," he said. "What is your request and it shall be granted,[54] if I am able to."

"Promise me, by your faith in the one you love most," she said.

"Yes, I promise," he said.

"I request that at the tournament you wear this sleeve on the pennon of your helmet, for the sake of my love."

When Lanç heard this he became extremely dejected. But because of the oath and pledge she had elicited from him, he was not permitted to refuse. Yet he was concerned about it, for he had already given his whole heart and desire to the Queen. He feared lest this matter ever be made known to her and she be angry and hate him.

[51] Cf. Proverbs 6:25, "Lust not after her beauty..."
[52] Cf. Judges 16:16. Delilah, trying to discover the secret of Samson's strength, "pressed him daily with her words."
[53] Cf. Esther 5:2 and 8:4, when Esther came unbidden to the King, he "stretched out" his sceptre to her.
[54] Cf. Esther 7:2, "What is your request and it shall be granted?" These words are addressed to Esther by King Ahasuerus.

ותקח הבתולה לפניו את בית זרועה ותקבעה בפנן אחד ותשימהו בידה על
אלמו ותצוהו לעשות בסיבוב נצחונות וגבורות על אהבתה בענן שכל הרואים
יאמרו כמה מאושרת וכמה מבורכת אותה הבית זרוע ומי אשר היא לה. וייודע
אליך אדוני כי אתה הוא הפרש הראשון אשר נתתי לו את חשקי וגם אליך
לא נתתיו לולי ידעתי אותך ואת גבורותיך.

ולנן ענה כי יעשה כל כך על אהבתה ששום איש לא יוכל להאשימו. וכבוא
השמש לקח רשות מן הבבסור ומן הגברת אשתו והפקידם לע|וליון| ואל
הבתולה השתחוה ואת מגיעו וזינו הניח שם בחדר אחד ואת הזינים האדומים
לבש כאמור לעיל. וירכבו שניהם הוא ואדלפרט ונושאי כליהם כל הלילה
עד הבוקר למען לא ינכרו מאיש. והגיעו עד פרסה סמוך לווינצשטרי טרם
עלות השמש אמ|רו| לנן אל אדלפרט חבירו היש מקום לחנות קרוב לעיר
כי איני בא לעיר היום ברצוני אם אוכל לחנות בחוץ.

ענהו אדלפרט טוב דברת הנה נלך אל מקום שייישר בעיניך עד מאד ותעבור
ותיכבד וילכו בכפר אחד סמוך לעיר בבית גברת אחת דודת אדלפרט הפרש
והגברת שמחה בהם ותקבלם בסבר פנים עד מאד ועמדו שם כל היום ההוא
בשמחה ובמשתה מכל מעדני מלך.

ותשאל הגברת אל נכדה על אודות חבירו מי הוא ויאמר לה איני יודע
מאודותיו דבר אבל נראה לי שהוא פרש אחד נכבד עד מאד ולכן נתחברתי
עמו ללכת אל הקיבוץ שלווינצשטרי. ולנן שלח את נערו לעיר ויצוהו לך
בעיר וראה הפרשים שבאו השוכנים תוך העיר והשוכנים מחוץ ותשום היטב
הכמות מן הפרשים שיש שם מפנים לעיר ומחוץ. ואנה חונים שני בורז
וליאונל ואחי אשטור.

40

The maiden took her sleeve, fastened it onto a pennon, then placed it on his helmet. She ordered him to be valiant and victorious in the tournament for the sake of her love, so that all beholders would say how happy and how blessed is that sleeve and the owner of it.

"May it be known to you, sir, that you are the first knight to whom I have given my desire. And I would not have given it to you had I not known of you and your valor."

Lanç replied that he would do so much for the sake of her love that no one could reproach him.

At sunset Lanç took leave of the vavasour and his wife, the lady, and recommended them to God. He bowed to the maiden, left his shield and armor in a room and donned the red armor mentioned above. He, Edelpert, and their armor-bearer rode throughout the night until morning so that they would not be recognized by any one. Just before sunrise, when they were about one mile from Wincestre, Lanç said to his friend Edelpert:

"Is there a place near the city where we can lodge? For I will not willingly enter the city if I can lodge outside it."

"Well said," answered Edelpert, "we shall go any place which pleases you most. You will go there and be honored."

They proceeded to a village near the city where a certain lady, an aunt of Edelpert, had a house. The lady rejoiced and welcomed them most graciously. They stayed there all that day, taking their delight in a feast fit for a king.

The lady asked her nephew who his friend was.

"I know nothing about him," he told her, "but it seems to me that he is a very highly honored knight, which is why I am accompanying him to the gathering at Wincestre."

Lanç sent his squire[55] to the city and commanded him: "Go about the city and survey the knights encamping inside the city and outside it. Carefully estimate the number of knights both inside and outside the city, and where my cousins Borz and Lionel and my brother Estor are encamping."

---

[55] Lit., "lad". See p. 47 for the scribe's word-choice for the actual term "squire".

לאלתר בא נערו העירה וראה וחקר כפי יכולתו כמות פרשי הקיבוץ ושהא
שם עד הערב ושב. ויאמר אל לנץ אדוני הפרשים רבים מפנים ומחוץ ושנייך
ואחיך הם בפנים וכן ראוי בעבור שהם מחבירי הטבלא ואי אפשר להם מבלי
היותם עם המלך ארטוש. שאל לנץ ומי ומי בחוץ.

ענה הנער עם רב ופרשים רבים עם ד' מלכים. מלך שקוציה מלך ארלנדי
מלך גליש מלך נורגוליש. אמנם פרשי מלכות לוגריש שהם עם המלך ארטוש
נראים אלי יותר פרשים נכבדים ויותר גיבורים גם אם החיצונים הם יותר
מספר. לבוקר הכינו וזיינו עצמם לנץ ורעהו וילכו אל הקיבוץ ונער לנץ
נשאר בכפר כי ירא לנץ פן יוכר הוא בעבור נערו ויהיו באחו שלוינצשטרי
והנה כולו מלא ומכוסה ממסבבים ועודרים.

ובו ביום לא אבה המלך ארטוש שמסיר גלון וגדריאט אחים ישאו כלי זיין
כי ידע שלנץ היה שם ולא אבה שיפגעו יחדיו למען לא תמצא ביניהם איבה.
והמלך עלה אל המגדל הוא וגלון וגדריאט ושאר פרשים כדי לראות הסיבוב
והסיבוב מתחיל להזדמן. ויאמר לנץ אל אדלפרט רעהו אל אי זו כת נראה
לך שנעזור הפנימים או החיצונים. ויען אדלפרט לאשר תחפוץ.

אמו|ר| לנץ נראה לי כי כי הפנימים הם חזקים וגיבורים מן החיצונים ולכן לא
יהיה לנו לכבוד אם נעזור או אם נהיה מצד החזקים. אמנם יגדל כבודנו
אם נעזור החיצונים שהם פחות גיבורים ובזה יוודע כוחנו ושוויינו. אז נתאמץ
לנץ על סוסו ויתיישר מול פרש אחד ויט חניתו ויכהו בחוזק יד[א] ויפילהו
ארצה הוא וסוסו ורכב לפנים כי עוד חניתו שלימה.

א· שמות יג,ג: כי בחוזק יד הוציא ה' אתכם מזה.

His squire left immediately for the city; he surveyed and investigated as best he could the number of knights at the gathering and remained there until evening, whereupon he returned.

"Sir," he said to Lanç, "there are many knights, both inside and out. Your cousins and your brother are inside. That then is seemly, for they are members of the Table and it would be impossible for them not to be with King Artus."

"And who is outside?" asked Lanç.

"Many people," the squire replied, "and many knights, including four kings: the King of Skoçia, the King of Erlandi, the King of Galis, and the King of Norgolis. But I think the knights of the Kingdom of Logris who are with King Artus are more noble and mighty, even though the ones outside are more numerous."

The next morning Lanç and his companion prepared and armed themselves and went to the tournament. Lanç's squire remained in the village, for Lanç feared he would be recognized because of his squire. They were in the plain of Wincestre which was entirely covered with jousters and contenders.

King Artus did not want the brothers Sir Galwan and Gadriat to bear arms that day, because he knew that Lanç was there and, so that there be no enmity between them, he did not want them to encounter each other.

The King, along with Galwan, Gadriat and the rest of the knights, went up to the tower in order to see the tournament, which began forthwith.

"Which group do you think we should help?" Lanç said to his companion Edelpert, "those inside or those outside?"

"Whichever you prefer," Edelpert replied.

"It seems to me," said Lanç, "that those inside are stronger and mightier than those outside; therefore it will not be to our honor if we help or join the stronger side. However, our honor will increase if we help the outside group, which is less strong, and thereby our strength and valor will be known."

Then Lanç braced himself on his horse and went directly toward one knight. He held his spear and struck him mightily,[56] felled horse and rider to the ground and, his spear remaining whole, rode

---

[56] Cf. Exodus 13:3-4. Lit., "with strength of hand."

ויפגע בפרש אחר ויעש לו ככה. וירכב לפנים ויפגע בשלישי ויעש לו ככה
אמנם את זה השלישי חבל מאד בצלעותיו חבלות גדולות ועמוקות וכמעט
מת. כראות פרשי המלך ארטוש גבורות זה הפרש תמהו מאד ויהללו את
גבורותיו ואמרו מה מאד התחיל לעשות היטב הפרש החדש כי הכל היו
סבורים שהיו שניהם אותם שני האחים מאשקלוט שנתפרשו באותה השנה
כאמור לעיל. עם היותם נושאים שניהם זינים אדומים מצבע אחד.

אז נעצרו יחד כת אחת מפרשים מיראתם את המכות שהיה מכה זה הפרש
האדום. ואדלפרט ריע לנץ פגע באשטור דמאריש אח מסיר לנץ ויכהו
בחניתו ואשטור נתאמץ עליו ביד רמה[א] והכהו בחניתו ודחקו כל כך בחזק
שהפילו לארץ עם סוסו ביחד. ויצעקו פרשי המלך ת|הילה| ל|אל| ח|י|
שעתה הותך אחד מפרשי אשקאלוט.

וכראות לנץ את רעהו נפול לארץ קינא לו קנאה גדולה וחרה לו עד מאד
ונתיישר מול אשטור ויט חניתו ויכהו מכה רבה ויפילהו לארץ לפני גאלאודין
דגאוליש וכמעט נתרסקו כל איבריו כי לא הכיר שהיה אשטור כי היו פניו
מכוסים מן האלמו והקפירון. ויאמר אל אדלפרט רעהו הנה נקמתי את
מפלתך. והתחזק והעלה את אדלפרט על הסוס והוציאו מתוך הפיכת
הפרשים.

אז אמ|ר| מסיר גלוון אל המלך לא אוכל להאמין שאותה ההכאה החזקה
אשר הפילה את אשטור יצאה מזרוע שום אחד מפרשי אשקאלוט החדשים
ואני חושב שאותו הפרש שעשאה הוא שום פרש אחד אכסנאי. ובורז בא
בתוך המערכה והחל להכות פרשים ולהפיל פרשים מימינו ומשמאלו כאילו

א. שמות יד,ח: ובני ישראל יוצאים ביד רמה.

on. He encountered another knight and did the same to him. He rode further and encountered a third and did the same, but this one he seriously wounded so deep in the ribs that he almost died.

When King Artus' knights saw the strength of this knight, they were quite astounded and praised his valor, saying:

"How well has this new knight begun."

For all thought that this pair were the brothers from Askalot who had become knights that year, since both were wearing red armor, as mentioned above.

Then, out of fear of the blows which the red knight dealt, one group of knights stayed together. Edelpert, Lanç' companion, encountered Estor de Mareis, Sir Lanç's brother, and struck him with his spear. Estor turned on him with upraised hand[57] and struck him with his spear with such force that he felled him and his horse to the ground.

The King's knights shouted, "Praised be the living God[58] that one of the knights of Askalot is now overthrown."

When Lanç saw that his friend was fallen to the ground, he was provoked into fierce rage. He set himself directly against Estor; he lifted his spear and struck several blows, felling him to the ground before Galaodin de Gaulis, so that all his limbs were well-nigh smashed. He did not recognize Estor because his face was covered with a helmet and a *capperone*.[59]

"I have now revenged your fall," he said to his companion Edelpert.

He braced himself and raised Edelpert up onto his horse and removed him from the melee of knights.

Then said Sir Galwan to the King:

"I cannot believe that the mighty blow which felled Estor came from the arm of any one of the new knights from Askalot. I think that the knight who did this is not a new knight at all."

Then Borz came into the fray and began to smite knights and fell them right and left as though they were all lambs, cleaving heads

---

[57] Cf. Exodus 14:8, "The Children of Israel went out with upraised hand."
[58] This phrase is a traditional Hebrew blessing. It does not occur in the O.F.
[59] The Cambridge Italian Dictionary defines *capperone* as "a peasant's hood worn over the cap."

הם כולם רחילים והיה הולם גולגולות ומשסע אלמים. פעם היה מכה בחנית וכאשר תישבר החנית היה מכה בחרב ועושה סביביו גבורות נפלאות.

וירא את לנץ וישמן אותו אך לא הכירו ויתייישר נוכחו ויט חניתו אחת עבה וקשה מול לנץ ויכהו ביד חזקה ובחפץ רב ויחלוף את מגן לנץ ואת שיריונו ותקע החנית בצלעותיו וחבל בו חבלות גדולות ועמוקות ודחקו כל כך בחנית עד שסוס ורוכבו[א] רמה לארץ רבת [77] אחת והדם היה מזנק ממנו עד מאד ומדמדם כל זיניו ובכן נשברה חנית בורז. ולנץ כפרש גיבור וחזק לא שכב לארץ ולא חשש על מכותיו ומיהר ועלה על סוסו בזדון גדול ובאחרי אף על חבלותיו ומפלתו.

ויאמר בקול נשמע חי ראשי זה שהפילני לארץ אותי ואת סוסי באחת איננו נער כי לא מצאתי מעולם מי שהכלימני שעשה לי בושה אחד לאלף כאשר עשה זה. אמנם לא עשה בימיו דבר שישולם גמולו מהר כאשר ישולם לו זה אם אם אוכל. לאלתר חשף חנית אחת חזקה מיד שקודיר אחד ונתייישר נגד בורז. וכראות פרשי הקיבוץ שאלה שני הפרשים נפגשים זה מול זה נסוגו כולם אחור ועשו להם מרחב גדול למען יוכלו להלחם היטב.

ויאמרו נראה מה יהיה כי עתה נלחמים יחדיו שני גיבורי עולם. כי שניהם גבורות נפלאות אמנם מי שינצח עתה אותו יהיה בודאי העליון מן הסיבוב ואליו יהיה הכבוד. אז נתאמץ לנץ על סוסו ויכה את בורז ביד חזקה ובחפץ גדול ובכעס ובחימה רבה בעניין שחשוקי האוכף שלבורז נשברו ובכן נפל לארץ והסוס הלך בשדה. ויאמר גלוון אל המלך אדוני מה תאמר מזה.

א׳   שמות טו,א: סום ורוכבו רמה בים.

and helmets. He struck with a spear, and when the spear broke, he wielded a sword, doing wondrous deeds of valor all around him.

He saw Lanç and marked him, but since he did not recognize him, he set out to slay him. He raised his thick, heavy spear at Lanç and struck him mightily, with great zeal. He pierced Lanç's shield and his coat of mail,[60] thrust deeply into his ribs and severely wounded him. He pressed him so hard with his spear that he felled both horse and rider[61] at once. Much blood spurted from him and it reddened all his armor. And thus Borz's spear broke.

Lanç, strong and valiant knight that he was, did not lie on the ground nor pay heed to his injuries, but hurriedly mounted his horse, full of zeal and wrath at his wounds and fall.

"By my head," he said loudly, "he who threw my horse and myself to the ground is no mere boy, for I have never found one among a thousand who has shamed and disgraced me as this one did, but he has never done anything which will be repaid so quickly as his deed now will be, if I am able."

He immediately drew a strong spear from the hand of a scudier[62] and went straight to Borz. When the knights of the tournament saw that these two knights were about to clash they all retreated and cleared a large space to enable them to fight better.

"Let us see what will happen," they said, "for now two of the world's heroes are about to fight, for both of them have done wondrous deeds of valor. But he who wins now will certainly be the mightiest of the tournament and to him will go all the glory."

Lanç braced himself on his horse and zealously struck Borz a mighty blow full of great anger and wrath, so that Borz's saddle-straps were broken and he fell to the ground, and his horse walked in the field.

Galwan said to the King: "Sir, what do you say to this?"

[60] Cf. I Samuel 17:5, referring to Goliath's coat of mail.
[61] Cf. Exodus 15:1, "The horse and his rider hath he thrown to the sea."
[62] The scribe, lacking a Hebrew equivalent for "squire," utilized the Italian word in his text.

47

אמר המלך ואתה מה תאמר. ענה גלוון איני דן מנותץ את בורז כפרש נפול
כי נפל מחמת שברון חשוקי האוכף ולא היה לו במה להיאחז. אמנם הפרש
האחר באמת הוא פרש טוב וחזק עד מאד ולולי שהנחנו את לנץ חולה
בקמלוט האמנתי שהוא לנץ.

והמלך שחק נגד גלוון ואמר אותו הפרש החל בטוב ואני סבור שישלים יותר
טוב ויהי מי /י/ודע שאם לא נשברו חשוקי האוכף כבר הטילו לארץ עם
הסוס אז חלפו מעבר אל עבר ולא הועילו שריונך. וכאשר נשברה חנית לנץ
שלף חרבו ויחל להכות מימינו ומשמאלו ולהפיל פרשים רבים זה אחר זה
כרחלים ולהתיז צוארי סוסים כדילועים ולעשות גבורות נפלאות בפלטיא עד
שהכל היו נפלאים . . .

48

"What do you say?" said the King.

Galwan answered: "I do not judge Borz to be a felled or over-thrown knight, since he fell on account of the broken saddlestraps which left him nothing to hold on to. But the other knight is truly an exceedingly strong and excellent knight. Had we not left Lanç sick at Camelot I would believe that this was Lanç."

The King smiled at Galwan and said: "That knight began well and I think that he will finish even better. Who knows but if the saddle-straps had not broken he would have already thrown him and his horse to the ground and pierced him through and through and then the coat of mail would not have helped him."

When Lanç's spear was broken he drew his sword and began to strike left and right, and fell many knights, one after another like lambs, and cut throats of horses like pumpkins, and to do wondrous deeds of valor in the field, so that all were amazed...[63]

why similies?

[63] For state of ms. at this point, see Introduction.

3

Literary Background of the Hebrew Arthurian Romance

Although it is fairly certain that the Hebrew manuscript is of Italian provenance, the author was not affected solely by literary taste and religious modes in Italy. As were the Italian Jews in general, so was the scribe influenced by the secular-literary culture of the Sephardic Jews of Spain and the anti-secular pietistic attitude of the Ashkenazic Jews of France and Germany. The intermingling of these two antipodal streams in the scribe's translation necessitates some remarks on the state of Hebrew letters in Europe during and preceding the thirteenth century.[1] The discussion will then proceed to the scribe's apology, which will be compared to the introductions to other secular Hebrew works.

In Spain, under the beneficial influence of Arabic literature, a tradition developed wherein secular literature was respected and accepted. As early as the eleventh century secular themes appeared in Hebrew poetry. The wealthy and influential Samuel Hanagid wrote battle poetry and love songs[2] and his more illustrious successors, such as Solomon ibn Gabirol, Judah Halevi and Moses ibn

---

[1] The comments will cover Hebrew literature in Spain (including Provence), Italy and Ashkenaz. In discussions of Hebrew literature, Provence is grouped with Spain because of their close cultural affinity, rather than with the rest of France. See Margolis and Marx, *History of the Jewish People*, Philadelphia, 1927, pp. 393 ff., and *infra* the title of Schirmann's anthology *Hebrew Poetry in Spain and Provence*. Ashkenaz comprises the Jewish settlement in middle and northern Europe; in this case northern France and Germany.

[2] *Diwan of Samuel Hanagid*, ed. D. S. Sassoon, London, 1934, pp. 7-11, and p. 92.

50

Ezra, added drinking songs and songs of friendship.[3] Not only a desire to emulate their Arab colleagues drove them to these artistic performances, but also a pride in the Hebrew language and a desire to show what feats it could accomplish stimulated many writers to try their hand at various literary forms.[4]

The Hebrew poetry of thirteenth century Spain and Provence,[5] which is richly variegated in content and form, contains sacred poetry as well as many secular genres.[6] Some poems are auto-biographical laments on the impoverished state of the poet,[7] others are polemics and poems of personal vituperation.[8] There also appear nature poems,[9] fables, and novella,[10] some akin in spirit to the erotic fabula that later appeared in Boccaccio and Chaucer.[11] In brief, as wide a selection as secular poetry permits was represented.

Typical of thirteenth century Spanish Jewish poets was Judah Al-Harizi (1165-1225). He translated parts of Maimonides' *Commentary* to the Mishna and his entire *Guide to the Perplexed* into Hebrew.[12] But his chief work was *Tahkemoni*, which might be called a picaresque novel in rhymed prose, influenced by an Arabic brand of adventure story known as the *maqama*.[13] Although Jewish authors of *maqamas* had didactic aims,[14] and although *Tahkemoni* contains biblical allusions, a satire on cantors which includes par-

---

[3] See their poetry in *An Anthology of Medieval Hebrew Literature*, ed. A. Millgram, New York, 1961, pp. 18-50.
[4] Salo Baron, *A Social and Religious History of the Jews*, 2nd ed., Phil., 1958, vol. vii, p. 159.
[5] See H. Schirmann's collection, *Hebrew Poetry in Spain and Provence* (Hebrew), Jerusalem-Tel-Aviv, 1960, vol. ii;
[6] Schirmann's anthology contains about one hundred different forms, many of them based on Arabic, Provençal and Greek models.
[7] *Ibid.*, p. 471, by Abraham Habedersi.
[8] *Ibid.*, p. 441, by Todros ben Yehuda Abulafia. Also, p. 334.
[9] *Ibid.*, pp. 299-300, by Meshalem ben Shlomo Diafara.
[10] *Ibid.*, p. 367 ff., "The Pious Man and his Wife the Adulteress." Although the framework is borrowed, the conversations are fully Jewish; laws and prayers are discussed in language spiced with biblical quotations.
[11] For instance, the adulterous wife theme that appears in the *Decameron*, Sixth Day, Seventh Tale, and Chaucer's "Merchant's Tale."
[12] Both appear in Maimonides *Guide*, tr. J. Al-Harizi, Warsaw, 1904.
[13] Judah Al-Harizi, *Tahkemoni*, ed. Y. Toporowski, Tel-Aviv, 1952.
[14] Baron, vii, 190.

odies of prayers, and a scene in Jerusalem mourning the ruins of Zion, Al-Harizi's work is essentially secular and contains many erotic passages.

Thirteenth century Spanish Jews were even ready for works devoted to love and sex, as is evidenced by the appearance of two works written by contemporaries of Al-Harizi. One was Yehuda ben Isaac Shabbetai's romance *Soneh Nashim* (The Misogynist), issued in 1208.[15] The story describes the adventures of a young man bidden by his father's dying command to remain single. The son tries to heed his father's will and departs with three companions for a distant land. However, his ideals of celibacy are soon shattered as he succumbs to a beautiful woman whom he seranades with love songs. Another writer whose work emphasized elements of sex and love was Jacob ben Eleazar (1170-1233), who translated into Hebrew the Arabic version of the Hindu fables *Kalilah V'Dimnah*.[16] His *Love Stories*[17] contain many sexual descriptions; one episode describes a couple who share a bed but do not touch; they sing songs of love to one another "until the fire of desire burned within them."[18]

In addition to secular works in Hebrew, thirteenth century Spanish Jews were also reading non-Hebraic secular literature. This fact is attested in the apology[19] to *Mashal ha-Kadmoni* (The Ancient Parable),[20] written by Yizhak ben Shlomo ibn Sahula

---

[15] *Soneh Nashim* of Yehuda Shabetai, ed. E. Ashkenazi, in *Taam Zkenim*, Frankfurt-am-Main, 1854, ff. 1-12.

[16] *Kalilah V'Dimnah*, tr. Jacob ben Eleazar, ed. Y. Dranburg, Paris, 1881.

[17] *The Love Stories* of Jacob ben Eleazar, ed. H. Schirmann, *Studies of the Research Institute for Hebrew Poetry in Jerusalem*, Vol. V, 1939, pp. 209-266.

[18] *Ibid.*, pp. 258-259. One of the ideals of love among the troubadors was the inflaming of desire up to the point of, but excluding, intercourse. See A. J. Denomy, *"Fin' Amors:* the Pure Love of the Troubadors, Its Amorality and Possible Source," *Med. Studies*, vol. VII (1945), p. 142. Jacob ben Eleazar, who lived after the early troubadors, may have been influenced by this concept. Denomy also suggests that among the intellectual currents which led to the development of courtly love was Arabic philosophy, and that Jews played an important role in the transmission of this knowledge from the Arabs to the Christians. See *ibid.*, p. 207, and also by Denomy, "An Inquiry into the Origins of Courtly Love," *Med. Studies*, vol. VI (1944), pp. 241-242.

[19] This apology is discussed below.

[20] Yizhak ben Shlomo ibn Sahula, *Mashal Ha-Kadmoni*, Tel Aviv, 1952.

(b. 1244). Here the author addresses himself to readers of non-sacred popular literature who read fables and parables in other languages and asserts that he wants to distract them from the "books of Homer and other pagans."[21]

Similar interest in literature outside the domain of the sacred is found in Italy, where the tradition of Hebrew letters was mainly under the influence of Spain.[22] During the twelfth century secular poetry appeared in Italy and worked its way up from the South to Rome, along with Spanish-influenced science and philosophy.[23]

By the thirteenth century, philosophy and poetry flourished in Italy beside a full range of Jewish studies. Contrary to Ashkenaz, in Spain and Italy "knowledge and religion met in peace."[24] In the latter, "zealous pietism found no nest."[25] So great was the desire for general knowledge among Italian Jews that even those who turned their backs on the new impetus toward learning fell unwillingly under its spell. The accent on liberal studies was also manifest in the education of the Italian-Jewish youth. In addition to Jewish studies, the older children received training in poetry, philosophy and all the natural sciences. The only fields of study excluded were theology and law; the first because it was entirely Christian, the second because Jews were not allowed to practice it. The discipline of talmudic studies, heavily weighted with legal procedure, served the Jews instead of law. While the Christian scholars practiced law, the Jewish scholars earned their living by practicing medicine.[26] The doctor-philosophers and the poet-grammarian-exegetes all had mastered talmudic and rabbinic literature.[27]

Not only was there influence of secular Hebrew culture from Spain upon the Italian Jews of the thirteenth century, but there was also much cross-fertilization between Christian and Jewish culture. For instance, at the beginning of the thirteenth century the Hebrew version of Maimonides' *Guide to the Perplexed* was translated by

---

[21] *Ibid.*, pp. 5-8.
[22] W. Chomsky, *Hebrew: The Eternal Language*, Phil., 1958, p. 179.
[23] Baron, vii, p. 176.
[24] M. Gudemann, *Jews in Italy* (Hebrew), Warsaw, 1898, vol. II, p. 161. Future references will be to "Gudeman *H.*"
[25] *Ibid.*, p. 112.   [26] *Ibid.*, p. 185.   [27] *Ibid.*, p. 91.

Christian scholars into Latin at the behest of Emperor Frederic II.[28] On the other hand, from the twelfth century on Jewish sages translated books of the scholastics into Hebrew,[29] and Jewish poets were influenced by their Christian contemporaries.[30]

The excursus into secular culture found notable expression in translations. Jews translated books of philosophy, astrology and geometry from Arabic into Hebrew,[31] but they were also involved in translations from Latin to Arabic. For their own use, Jews sometimes translated from Latin to Hebrew,[32] as for instance Hillel ben Samuel, who translated several medical treatises from Latin to Hebrew.[33]

In addition to translation from scholarly works, the Italian Jews of the thirteenth century wrote original secular works of many types. An anthology devoted to Hebrew poetry in Italy shows the scope of these diverse genres. Included are maqamas,[34] elegies,[35] meditations,[36] humorous and sarcastic songs,[37] songs of passion,[38] panegyrics,[39] and poems on historic events.[40] Even a work of

[28] M. Steinschneider, *Hebraeischen Uebersetzungen*, Berlin, 1893, p. 433, states that a manuscript of the *Guide* in Latin was located in the Munich Library.
[29] Berakya Hanakdan's translation of *Questiones Naturales* by Adelard of Bath (1120) was called *Dodi V'Nekdi*, London, 1920. Also, in his collection of essays on the Pentateuch, Jacob Anatoli, (c. 1200-1250) *Malmad ha-Talmidim*, Lyck, 1866, quotes extensively from the works of Michael Scotus, a Christian scholar.
[30] For instance, Immanuel of Rome, a friend of Dante, wrote sonnets in Hebrew in the latter part of the thirteenth century.
[31] Gudemann, *H.*, p. 133. Moreover, there existed a group of Jewish scholars in Rome who out of love for learning copied many scientific manuscripts in order to satisfy the great demand for books. See Tsinberg, i, p. 327 and Gudemann, *H.*, ii, p. 111.
[32] Cecil Roth, *History of the Jews in Italy*, Phil., 1946, p. 148.
[33] H. Vogelstein and P. Rieger, *Geschichte der Juden in Rom*, Berlin, 1896, pp. 402-403.
[34] H. Schirmann, *Anthology of Hebrew Poetry in Italy* (*Hebrew*), Berlin, 1934, p. 88, by Benjamin belli Mansi, and p. 137, by Immanuel of Rome.
[35] *Ibid.*, p. 119, by Yehiel ben Yekutiel, and p. 164, by Immanuel of Rome.
[36] *Ibid.*, p. 121, by Yehiel ben Yekutiel, and p. 165, by Immanuel of Rome.
[37] *Ibid.*, p. 127, by Hillel ben Samuel, and pp. 127, 137, 145, by Immanuel of Rome.
[38] *Ibid.*, pp. 159-162, by Immanuel of Rome.
[39] *Ibid.*, p. 152, by Immanuel of Rome.
[40] *Ibid.*, p. 100, by Zedekiah ben Benjamin.

ethics, whose ostensible purpose was not diversion but moral better-
ment, shows the influence of secular literature. Almost contemporaneous with the Hebrew Arthurian romance of 1279, *Maalot ha-
Midot*[41] (Attributes of Ethics) by R. Yehiel ben Yekutiel was written
in 1278. Although the author is presenting moral instruction, he
does not hesitate to quote from such non-Jewish sources as the
Sages of Rome,[42] the sayings of Alexander of Macedon,[43] and
Aristotle,[44] and even a parable by Emperor Frederic II.[45]

The flourishing of Hebrew secular literature during the thirteenth
century, the thorough Jewish and general education of Italian Jews
and the scholarly contacts between Christians and Jews combined to
make possible the translation of an Arthurian romance into Hebrew.
By 1279 Hebrew secularism had been entrenched so firmly that the
appearance of an Arthurian romance probably did not come as a
shock to readers of Hebrew. Nevertheless, it could not have
appeared without an apology of some sort, for the influence upon
the translator did not stem only from literary conditions in Italy:
to a degree, the warmth of the apology and the translator's treatment of his text to minimize its secularity point to a subtle religious
influence from Franco-German Jewry.

Non-sacred writing in Hebrew had a different history in the
Ashkenazic community from that in Spain and Italy. Whereas
before and during the thirteenth century in the latter centers
learned Jews produced sacred and secular works, in Ashkenaz the
intelligentsia was preoccupied only with Torah study. Here a translation of an Arthurian romance would have been highly improbable.
The sole attempts at secular Hebraic composition were some
chronicles which recorded the Ashkenazic Jews' suffering and
oppression during the Crusades.[46] However, despite the lack of
Jewish creativity in the secular fields, evidence exists that the
Ashkenazic Jews were at least reading non-sacred literature in the
vernacular. This information, originating from comments and interdicts concerning literature in the vernacular, sheds light not only on

[41] Yehiel ben Yekutiel, *Maalot ha-Midot*, Warsaw, 1876.
[42] *Ibid.*, p. 100.   [43] *Ibid.*, p. 98.
[44] *Ibid.*, p. 16.   [45] *Ibid.*, p. 51.
[46] Y. Baer, p. 288, "Secular Literature of German and French Jewry,"
(Hebrew) *Sinai*, Vol. 16, Jerusalem, 1953.

the literary interests of the Jews in Ashkenaz but also, as will be shown below, on the scribe's composition of a secular work in non-Ashkenazic Italy.

An authoritative Ashkenazic guidebook from the beginning of the thirteenth century, *Sefer Hasidim* (Book of the Pious), attributed to Judah of Regensburg, prohibited Jews from using romances for binding purposes.[47] To be read in conjunction with this remark is a contemporaneous statement of R. Judah of Paris (1166-1244), in the Commentary to the Talmud of the Tosafists,[48] forbidding both on Sabbath and weekdays the reading of "those tales of battles written in the vernacular."[49]

Since an interdict usually shows that the censured act is being performed, R. Judah's proscription can serve to indicate the popularity of non-Hebraic writing. But contact with outside literature evidently was not a new phenomenon. Already in the twelfth century Jews were reading love songs and ballads;[50] in fact, during the twelfth century and the early part of the thirteenth the literature of romantic love actually influenced the behavior of some Jews.[51]

The common folk were not the only ones touched by this non-sacred literature. Even the rabbis themselves fell victim to its charms. The statement in *Sefer Hasidim* forbidding the covering of sacred books with romances which were "worthless matters concerning the conflicts of kings,"[52] reveals more than the fact that romances were circulating; it shows that the stories were also read by the very authorities who prohibited them, as does R. Judah's

---

[47] *Sefer Hasidim*, ed. R. Margoliot, Jerusalem, 1958, Sect. 141.

[48] The Tosafists were scholars of the Franco-German academies; they flourished from the eleventh to the mid-fourteenth centuries. See M. Waxman, *History of Jewish Literature*, Vol. I, New York, 1960, pp. 268 ff.

[49] Tosafot Sabbath 116 b.

[50] Gudemann *H.*, i, p. 32.

[51] Monford Harris, *"Concept of Love in Sefer Hasidim,"* *Jewish Quarterly Review*, Vol. 50, 1959, pp. 313 ff. The author suggests that current conceptions of courtly love influenced the citation in *Sefer Hasidim* which concerned Jewish men and women who proceeded in love play merely for the sake of inflaming desire without its consummation.

[52] *Sefer Hasidim*, Sect. 141.

description of the romances: "Those tales of battles written in the vernacular."[53]

A fascinating glimpse into the worldly knowledge of readers of sacred literature is also given by an early thirteenth century French exegete, R. Isaac ben R. Judah Halevi. In seeking to explain the angel's refusal to reveal his name to Jacob, R. Isaac cites the tournaments where "the victor asks the name of the defeated, in order to boast in that city, and the defeated refuses for this very reason."[54] Another French exegete, Rashi's noted grandson, R. Samuel b. Meir (died 1174), also betrays his knowledge of secular literature when he compares the exchanges of the lovers in the *Song of Songs* to the ballads of the troubadors: "Even today they sing their love songs in this manner – where the roles are divided between the lovers."[55]

The influence of the two aforementioned prohibitions of Ashkenazic rabbis was no doubt felt in non-Ashkenazic Italy because of the contact between the two Jewries. We find, on the one hand, that even before 1300 there were some communities of Ashkenazic Jews in the Venetian republic;[56] and on the other, that Italian scholars consulted the rabbis of France and Germany, and Italian students were sent to the Ashkenazic academies.[57]

Because of the religious contact between Ashkenazic and Italian Jewries and the Jewish education of Italian Jews, the Hebrew scribe was presumably aware of these interdicts by the Ashkenazic authorities. Similarly, he was in all likelihood familiar with the statement of Maimonides, the great Sephardic authority revered in Spain and Italy, who cautioned his readers that it was a "sheer waste of time" to read any of the histories of the Arabs "or books of song and similar works, which neither possess wisdom nor benefit anybody."[58]

---

[53] Tosafot Sabbath 116b.
[54] Isaac ben R. Judah Halevi, *Paaneah Raza*, Commentary to Genesis 32:30, Tarnopol, 1803.
[55] Samuel ben Meir, *Commentary to the Song of Songs*, 3:5, Leipzig, 1855.
[56] M. Shulvass, *Jewish Life in Italy during the Renaissance* (Hebrew), N. Y., 1955, p. 5.
[57] Gudemann, *H.*, ii, p. 169.
[58] Maimonides, *Commentary to Sanhedrin*, ch. x, 1, Slavita, 1830.

But knowledge of an interdict does not necessarily mean compliance. The translator, who himself read romances, may have been more cognizant of the interdict when he set out to write a romance than when he was reading one. Perhaps he rationalized that if he read romances, the burden of disobedience was on him alone, but that if he wrote them, he would cause a host of people to transgress. Despite the fact that there was precedent for secular and even erotic themes in Hebrew, a combination of the scribe's own personal piety and the Ashkenazic and Sephardic prohibitions no doubt played an important role in the scribe's elaborate defense. His apology may be better understood when compared with apologies to some other works which appeared in Spain and Italy. All these reveal their respective authors' approaches and attitudes towards secular writing.

Jacob ben Eleazar (1170-1233) prefaces his *Love Stories* by stating that he wrote his book because the Arabs had denigrated Hebrew and mocked the Jews. He seeks to disprove the accusation and show the capacity of the sacred tongue, Hebrew,[59] but he makes no effort to disguise the obvious references to sex in his stories, or even to excuse them on didactic grounds. A similar approach is offered by Al-Harizi (1165-1225), the author of *Tahkemoni*. He too introduces his work with the statement that he is writing to show that "the Hebrew language is unrivalled in clarity of expression and the beauty of its parables."[60] In neither of the above works does the apology give any hint of the intention to improve morally.

Although in his apology to *Mashal ha-Kadmoni*, Ibn Sahula (b. 1244) also accents the power of the Hebrew language, his purpose is to wean Hebrew readers away from foreign authors and to draw them back to Hebrew, and, eventually, to the Torah and holy lore. That is why he has the animals in his fables quote the Torah and Talmud to support their arguments. For, as he tells us, he does not have to imitate the Arabic writers, since the Bible contains sufficient parables to serve him as models.[61] Ibn Sahula, then, goes further than the other two authors in adducing for his work a didactic

---

[59] Jacob ben Eleazar, op. cit., p. 212.
[60] Al-Harizi, op. cit., p. 5.
[61] Ibn Sahula, op. cit., pp. 5-8.

58

element. In contrast, the preface of a non-secular ethical work such as Yehiel ben Yekutiel's *Maalot ha-Midot* (1278) does not have to laud the power of the Hebrew language, for it is being applied in devout fashion. However, the work does show the inroads which secular culture had made even into a Hebrew work of moral instruction. Since the Italian author lived in an age which in addition to religious studies had accepted secular subjects, he feels obliged to include some parables and ethical teachings of gentile sages and philosophers, explaining in his apology that he does so "in order to attract young men to his work."[62]

Comparing these apologies to the one penned by the Hebrew scribe, we see a marked difference in approach. The preceding apologies attached to secular works reveal that where the work was essentially for diversion (*Tahkemoni, Love Stories*), the authors were mainly concerned with defending the Hebrew language; where the contents were entertaining but also didactic (*Maalot ha-Midot*), the apology was actually a reflection of the contents. But in the Hebrew romance the essential nature of the contents – two adulterous relationships and at least one recognizable Christian scene – was really at odds with the pious apology. Even the erotic episodes are for the scribe converted to lessons in morality. Therefore, whereas some of the others were writing for the glory of the language, the scribe's ultimate purpose was, or perforce had to be, the glory of God.

Nevertheless, since apologies were usually prefixed to longer works, the problem of determining the balance between sincere piety and conventional literary form in the apology should be examined. The amount of secular Hebrew writing in Spain and Italy prior to the Hebrew Arthurian translation of 1279 clearly indicates that the use of Hebrew was not solely reserved for sacred compositions. The education which the scribe presumably received consisted of secular and Hebrew studies. Indeed his translation alone shows us his familiarity with Jewish learning[63] and with various Arthurian romances.[64] His brief omissions of Christian matter, such as Lancelot's visit to a monk to say Mass, the suppression of Uter's

---

[62] Yehiel ben Yekutiel, *Maalot ha-Midot*, Warsaw, 1876, p. 2.
[63] See Translation, pp. 11, 13.
[64] *Ibid.*, pp. 15 and 29.

Christmas feast and the allusion, via biblical verses, to a feast from the Bible,[65] show that the scribe was cognizant of Christian coloration; very likely he was also aware of the Christian nature of the grail and hence his choice of a specifically Jewish term for dish to disguise it.[66] Coupled with this was the fact that he was no doubt aware of the various interdicts against romances. He may have balanced prohibitions against romance with the already established tradition of secular Hebrew writing. The latter may have given him the impetus to make his translation, whereas the interdicts, the secular nature of the romance, as well as his own piety, probably prompted the fervent tone of his apology.

The scribe gives two reasons for undertaking the translation. He states that one reason was to drive away melancholy, but implies by his hint at a rabbinic commentary,[67] by calling upon the good name of R. Johanan ben Zakkai,[68] and by mentioning the tales read to the High Priest on the eve of the Day of Atonement,[69] that diversion is only a temporary means to a higher sacred purpose. But the more important reason for his translation was that sinners might repent and return to God.[70] None of the other previously cited apologies to secular works make of their compositions a vehicle for sinners' path to repentance. The Jewish references in the apology and the many biblical allusions in the text reveal that the scribe was consistent in his aim. There is little reason, then, to believe that the tone of the apology is conventional or insincere; the *fact* of the apology may have been predetermined, but the scribe used a conventional instrument to express his avowed pious intent.

[65] *Ibid.*, p. 17.
[67] *Ibid.*, p. 11.
[69] *Ibid.*, p. 13.

[66] *Ibid.*, p. 25.
[68] *Ibid.*, p. 11.
[70] *Ibid.*, p. 13.

4

Jewish Aspects of the Hebrew
Arthurian Romance

The truth of the statement that every translation is in a sense a commentary is apparent in the Hebrew version of the Arthurian romance, where the scribe has not only translated the stories but judaized them as well. Evidently determined to make the romance sound as Jewish as possible, the translator utilizes biblical phraseology and other terms which readily suggest Jewish associations to the reader. Moreover, the scribe's moral approach to the romance, as well as his various departures (despite his use of an Italian version) from the traditional Old French text, also help to enhance the Jewish coloration.

The scribe's method of judaization is evident at the outset of the romance, for the apology itself is filled with terms from a familiar Jewish world. Various citations from the Bible, Mishna and Talmud are used to support the reading of fables, apparently to convince the reader who might possibly hesitate to indulge in non-sacred material. R. Johanan ben Zakkai and his knowledge of fox fables,[1] the rabbinic commentary on the beneficial uses of a minstrel,[2] the tales read to the High Priest,[3] are all mentioned for the express purpose of establishing the permissibility of the Hebrew translation. However, it is the conclusion of the apology which contains the scribe's most cogent argument: the tale offers practical morality. Sinners will learn to repent and return to God. The scribe intends, then, for his translation to serve as a secular sermon.

[1] See Translation, p. 11.
[2] Tr., p. 11.   [3] Tr., p. 13.

In order to achieve his intended purpose, the scribe handles the material before him in a special manner. His choice of plot, additions and omissions, use of language, and treatment of certain passages to accent Jewish ideas, are all instrumental in the judaization of the Arthurian romance.

To make his translation more palatable to Jewish readers, the scribe may purposely have chosen to begin with the Uter-Izerna theme, whose plot has a striking affinity to the biblical story concerning David, Bathsheba and Uriah. A Jew familiar with the Bible could hardly have failed to note the parallels.[4] In both cases a king falls in love with a married woman; he desires her and sleeps with her; the husband of the married woman is killed in battle, which enables the king to marry the already pregnant woman. Both women also bear a future king. The motif of the woman who thinks she is sleeping with her husband, lacking in the biblical story, may have prompted the Hebrew readers to recall Rashi's exposition on Exodus 2:11, where an Egyptian taskmaster desires the wife of a Hebrew slave, calls out the slave at night and enters, sleeping with the woman who thinks it is her husband who has returned.

The scribe need not have chosen the Uter-Izerna episode because of its titillating story or because this was the only tale at his disposal. After all, we gather from his translation that he was also familiar with the prose *Lancelot*,[5] yet he did not translate any of those adventures.

Whereas the first episode resembled the plot of a famous Jewish story and was useful from the point of view of holding the Hebrew reader's attention, the second episode, that from the *Mort Artu*, was suitable for its theme, one admirably pertinent to the scribe's moralistic approach. In fact, that theme, which he spells out explicitly for his audience, may be the very reason why he chose to translate the *Mort Artu*. The statement that "this evil desire [of Lancelot and Artus' wife, Zinevra] was the cause of the destruction of the Table, the death of King Artus and the ruin of the Kingdom"[6]

---

[4] Perhaps the mention of David (Tr. p. 13) could have aided the reader's pattern of association.

[5] See Tr. pp. 15 and 29.

[6] Tr., p. 29.

could presumably affect the reader. He might hold in abeyance any admiration of Lancelot and Zinevra and be reminded of the Jewish world view of a God, the agent of history, who punishes the guilty and rewards the righteous. Perhaps the scribe inserted a thematic summary at this point because he himself had been excessively enthusiastic about the Lancelot-Zinevra affair.

A few lines before the statement of the theme the scribe had inserted the remark "strong as death is love"[7] to explain, perhaps to excuse, Zinevra's passion. This quotation from the biblical ode to love, the Song of Songs, is not found in the Old French version and, though possibly taken from the lost Italian source, is more likely an addition of the Hebrew scribe. Yet this is a puzzling insertion, for the scribe seemingly uses a biblical proof text to explain an act forbidden by Jewish law. Perhaps he realized what he had done by adding the biblical phrase and, to counteract it, provided the statement of the theme. One can almost see the change of heart which comes over the scribe in the few lines between his excuse for Zinevra's behavior, to the point when he returns to the biblical theme of Deuteronomy and the prophets: sin is the cause of destruction.

To the broader Jewish aspects of plot and theme the scribe introduces Jewish tonal color by various effective additions to and omissions from the text. When Uter Pendragon tells Izerna that the child will be named Artusin because he was born through the power of art,[8] the King is following biblical precedent. Naming a child for a certain reason is traditional in the Bible; moreover, there is usually some etyomological, or pseudo-etymological connection between the name and the event, as there is with Artus.

Further evidence of judaizing occurs throughout the text. During a love speech Lancelot makes use of the term "Ha-shem"

---

[7] Tr., p. 27.

[8] Tr. p. 23. R. S. Loomis, *Celtic Myth and Arthurian Romance*, New York, 1927, p. 34, says that along with the Jews, the Welsh also showed an aptitude for explaining names in their stories. The Bretons and the French took over this tradition for seeking etymologies. However, since the biblical mode of naming is the most ancient, and since no reason is given for Artus' name in the O.F., we may assume that the Hebrew scribe, working from his own tradition, originated the etymology for Artus' name.

(the Name),[9] which is the way that a pious Jew refers to God without mentioning the Divine name in vain. In another passage, during the height of the jousting, the knights shout, "Praised be the living God."[10] Bizarre as Lancelot's Jewish piety and the Christian knights' Jewish blessing may seem, they add the details that help strengthen the Jewish elements of the romance.

Although a thirteenth century Jewish reader was probably oblivious of the slight editing done by the Hebrew scribe, some of the changes and omissions fit into his pattern of weakening or suppressing Christian elements. One such omission appears in the Lancelot fragment, which follows the traditional Old French version more closely than does the Uter-Izerna episode. In Lancelot's visit to Edelpert's aunt, a brief interlude is missing in the Hebrew. From the scribe's Jewish point of view the omission is readily understandable, for those lines tell how Lancelot goes to hear Mass and offer his prayers as befits a Christian knight.[11]

A second omission occurs when the son of Uter and Izerna is given his name. In the Hebrew text the child is named "Artusin, that is, born through the power of art."[12] Whereas in the Hebrew Artus is named after an event in the biblical manner, in the O.F. Artus is baptized,[13] and hence the scribe's omission of this Christian rite.

A third omission is found in the Uter fragment. According to the French sources the occasion at which Uter meets Igraine is a Christmas feast.[14] In the Hebrew version, however, the scribe makes no mention of Christmas.[15] On the contrary, Uter's feast is described in the language of Ahasuerus' feast in the book of Esther. The scribe tells how the king made a great feast for all the people and all the princes (Va-ya'as ha-melech mishteh gadol l'chol

[9] Tr. p. 33.   [10] Tr., p. 45.

[11] See *Mort Artu*, ed. J. Frappier, Paris, 1956, p. 12. "Et l'endemain, si tost comme li jorz aparut, se leva Lancelos et ala oir messe a la chapele a un hermite qui pres d'ilec estoit herbergiez en un boscage. Quant il ot messe oie et ie ot fetes ses oroisons, einsi comme chevaliers crestiens doit fere..."

[12] See Tr., p. 23.

[13] *Vulgate Version of the Arthurian Romance*, ed. H. O. Sommer, Washington, 1908, vol. ii, p. 76. "& cil respont se tu le ueus baptisier a ma uolonte & a mon los il aura a non artus."

[14] *Ibid.*, p. 58.   [15] Tr., p. 17.

ha'amim v'hasarim). Concerning Ahasuerus, the Bible relates: "The king made a great feast for all his princes and servants."[16] (Va-ya'as ha-melech mishteh gadol l'chol sarav v'avadav). Besides the substitution of "people" for "servants," the only difference between the scribe's Hebrew and the biblical verse is in the last two nouns, which in the Arthurian Hebrew text are in the nominative and in the Bible in the possessive case. Through the scribe's omission of some details from the Arthurian text and careful choice of words, he has managed to change a Christmas feast into what might be called a Purim feast. The scribe thus not only judaizes by using biblical language to suppress a Christian element, but by means of biblical phraseology he also directs the Jewish reader's attention to various biblical stories. These linguistic elements scattered throughout the text enhance the general Jewish character of the romance.

Although in the process of translation the scribe often chooses the biblical word, two "Jewish" terms were included in the romance without premeditation, for they appeared in the original. Encountering the phrase "scions of the house of David" (zera beit David)[17] at the outset of the romance, the reader would feel a ready sense of identification, for many of the noblest Jews, a dynasty of rabbis of the Talmud, as well as the leaders of Babylonian Jewry, traced their descent to the house of David, a lineage considered to be of the highest distinction. Another word found in the French and the Hebrew texts which yields rich symbolic association for a Jewish reader is "Jerusalem."[18] Although in the O.F. "Jerusalem" is used as an image for a distant place,[19] for the Hebrew reader Jerusalem is not far at all; perhaps no further than his heart, or his prayerbook, with its many passages supplicating for the rebuilding of Jerusalem and for the return of God's glory to Zion. The mention in the text of this word so fraught with religious-national connotations can be considered another example of a Jewish element in the text which aids the Hebrew reader in accepting the romance.

[16] Esther 2:18.
[17] Tr., p. 13, and Sommer, op. cit., vol. iii, p. 13, "comme chele qui est deschendre de la haute lignie le roi david."
[18] Tr., p. 23.
[19] *Mort Artu*, op. cit., p. 1, "de si lointeingnes terres comme sont les parties de Jerusalem."

Moreover, because of its strong religious significance, recall of Jerusalem could conceivably add to the process whereby "sinners will learn the path of repentance and return to the Name (i.e., God)".[20]

With "scions of the House of David" and "Jerusalem" the scribe was fortunately presented with two terms which helped him in his general pattern of judaizing the text. However, he added many more on his own. The opening words of the romance lead the reader into a biblical world. "This is the history of Sir Lancelot" (lit. "these are the generations of..."),[21] the standard opening for a biblical epic: so begin the stories of Noah, Shem, Isaac, and Jacob[22] (in Hebrew: eyle toldot), is premiditated, for he had recourse to other Hebrew introductory phrases of this sort. Indeed he utilizes an alternate phrase in introducing the Uter episode: "the order of the history (lit. the generations) of Artus" (seder toldot)[23] – a phrase which is not found in the Bible.

Following close upon the biblical beginning "these are the generations of" comes the previously cited phrase "the scions of the House of David" and the oft-repeated phrase "it is not written?",[24] the traditional mode of cross reference in the Bible. After the first few lines of the text, then, the reader has already had his Jewish sensibilities stimulated.

These first three biblical citations have really set the groundwork, for they have introduced the reader to a biblical mood and mode of thought. The language has not as yet made him recall any specific biblical scenes. But this process begins forthwith and does not cease until the end of the romance.

When Uter becomes ill out of love for Izerna, the scribe uses the biblical word which describes Amnon's illness caused by his passion for Tamar.[25] The word "to become ill" (l'hitchalot) appears in the Bible only once, and both in the Bible and in the romance it is used to describe men who become ill out of a desire for a woman normally forbidden to them. Such precision in language occurs a number of

[20] Tr., p. 13.   [21] *Ibid.*
[22] Genesis 6:9, 11:10, 25:19, 37:2. "Eyle toldot Noah..."
[23] Tr., p. 15.   [24] Tr., p. 15.
[25] II Samuel 13:2. The words cited as *hapax logomena* appear nowhere else in classical Hebrew.

times. For instance when the Maid of Askalot seeks information about Lancelot's identity from his armor bearer, the scribe says "she strongly pressed" (va'te'elatz) him.[26] The only time this word appears in the Bible is in the verse describing how Delilah "strongly pressed" Samson to reveal the secret of his strength; both in the Bible and in the romance women seek information from reluctant men.

The scribe has already prompted the reader to recall the Samson story. At the beginning of the narrative when Uter begs Merlin for help, he says, "Pray help me only this time"[27] (azreyni nah ach ha-pa'am), an easily recognizable paraphrase of a popular biblical verse, "Pray strengthen me only this time"[28] (chazkeyni nah ach ha-pa'am), which is Samson's prayer as he stands, blind, between the pillars of the Philistine temple. The Samson element is utilized for a third time in the scene where Lancelot and Edelpert depart for the tournament. Referring to Lancelot's reticence in revealing his identity to Edelpert, the scribe tells us, "he did not tell him his name" (V'et shmo lo higid lo).[29] The biblical verse relating the encounter of Samson's mother with the man of God, who also refuses to give his name, reads: "He did not tell me his name" (V'et shmo lo higid li).[30] The sense of mystery suggested in the Hebrew by a man of God refusing to give his name[31] could presumably make the reader view Lancelot as a knight endowed with some measure of suprahuman invincibility. Yet at the very same time the verse draws the reader's attention to a biblical encounter.

Another instance of careful attention to word choice occurs in the scene where Artus notes that forty-two of his men "were missing"[32] (nifkdu), having died in the war of the Quest. The Hebrew word (with a slight variation in grammatical aspect) is the one used to describe the men David lost in a certain battle. This particular verb for missing men occurs twice in the Bible (II Samuel 2:30, va-yipakdu, and Numbers 31:49, nifkad), and in both cases it is used in the sense of men missing in battle.

[26] Tr., p. 39, and Judges 16:16.
[27] Tr., p. 19. [28] Judges 16:28. [29] Tr., p. 37.
[30] Judges 13:7.
[31] See also Genesis 32:30, where the angel refuses to reveal his name to Jacob after having struggled with him. [32] Tr., p. 25.

When Artus expresses his sorrow over the loss of Bano of Magoç, he says, "My heart grieves"[33] (al zeh dahveh libi). Although there are other expressions for sadness available in Hebrew, the scribe bases his phrase upon one which occurs at the conclusion of Lamentations: "Our heart grieves for this" (al zeh dahveh libenu).[34] This biblical text, traditionally recited at sad occasions, mourns the destruction of Jerusalem and the Temple. Of course there is nothing original here in the expression of grief, but the use of a close paraphrase of this particular passage, which occurs only once in the Bible, against thrusts the reader into a Jewish frame of reference at the very moment he is experiencing a scene in the romance. In other words, the Hebrew term the scribe uses is heavily weighted and can affect the reader's sensibilities, whereas another more 'neutral' word might not have done so.

Sadness is also brought into play as Izerna mourns the death of her husband. Attempting to estimate how far her husband had gone, Izerna uses the expression "bowshot's distance"[35] (harchek kim'tachavey keshet), a phrase which occurs only once in the Bible, in the Abraham-Hagar story. After Abraham had expelled Hagar and her son Ishmael from the house, Hagar wandered in the wilderness until her water supply was exhausted. She then placed her child under some shrubbery and moved a bowshot's distance away (harchek kim'tachavey keshet)[36] because she did not want to see him die. Then she sat down and wept. Here again there is a certain similarity of theme. The special phrase weds the two situations, in both of which a wronged woman is mourning the loss of a beloved person. As the Hebrew reader encounters the phrase, he is prompted to see an Arthurian incident against the backdrop of a biblical scene.

In certain passages, then, the scribe appears to be using the language for two different ends. On the narrative level he tells a romance; yet when his narrative is broken up into smaller elements, it suggests completely different situations. A good example of this occurs when the Maid of Askolot begins to ask Lancelot that he wear her sleeve. Lancelot rises, stretches out (Vayoshet) his hand and says that her request will be granted (ma sh'elatech v'tinaten

[33] Tr., p. 25. [34] Lamentations 5:17.
[35] Tr., p. 19. [36] Genesis 21:16.

lach).[37] In one respect the language serves the purpose of moving the narrative forward, of describing Lancelot's deeds and words. However, the phrases in the Hebrew echo the popular Esther story where the young Queen requests King Ahasuerus to save her people, and immediately invest Lancelot and the Maid for a moment with biblical dress. In the Bible Ahasuerus stretches out (Vayoshet) his sceptre to the Queen and tells her that her request will be granted (ma sh'elatech v'tinaten lach).[38] Once again, because of the suggestive power of certain words which the reader easily recognizes, the Hebrew serves the purpose of reminding him of Jewish situations.

The magic of association which transforms a scene from the romance into a biblical incident also occurs in the battle scene. The few key phrases from the Bible which are used to describe knightly victories make the reader recall Israelite battles as described in the Bible. Within the space of a few lines there appear in the text three famous phrases from Exodus which describe the victory of the Israelites over the Egyptian hosts. That God took Israel out of slavery "with strength of hand"[39] (B'chozek yad) and "with upraised hand"[40] (b'yad ramah) is repeated many times. (A variation of "with strength of hand" – "with strong hand" (b'yad chazakah) – occurs even more frequently in the Bible,[41] and is quoted in the daily prayers and in the Passover service.) Moses' Song of Victory recounts twice that God's might has overthrown the "horse and rider"[42] (sus v'rochbo) of the Egyptians; and the Song of Miriam takes up this line as a refrain. Since the entire Song of Moses is included in the daily morning service, the Jewish associations of these terms are assured.

An example of a phrase in the text which not only prompts Jewish associations but also contains moralistic overtones appears in the scribe's depiction of the Maid of Askolot's inner feeling, "in her heart she lusted for Lanç' beauty"[43] (vatachmod bi'lvava et yofi Lanç).

[37] Tr., p. 39.
[38] Esther 5:2 and 8:4, and 7:2.
[39] Tr., p. 43, and Exodus 13:3-4.
[40] Tr., p. 45, and Exodus 14:8.
[41] Exodus 6:1, 13:9, 32:11; Deut. 9:26; Ezekiel 20:33.
[42] Tr., p. 47, and Exodus 15:1.
[43] Tr., p. 39.

69

While the Hebrew scribe relates how the Maid was attempting to seduce Lancelot, the phrase calls attention to the opening verse of a section in Proverbs 6:25: "Lust not after her beauty in your heart" (Al tachmod yofya bi'lvavecha), which initiates a ten-verse admonition against association with harlots and married women. As the narrative is propelled forward by telling of the Maid's desire for Lancelot, the paraphrase of the Proverbs verse brings to mind the biblical warning against promiscuity.

This manner of narration is fully in line with the scribe's stated intent that a "sinner will learn the paths of repentance"[44] and imbue himself with ethics and wisdom.[45] Any Hebrew reader who recalled the subsequent verses in Proverbs about the immorality and the dangers of adultery might very well be forced to consider the situation of Lancelot and make a moral judgment on him.

Although not every word in the Hebrew text is fraught with rich associations, the key phrases that do appear draw the reader's attention back to a Jewish story. It might also be said that the Hebrew version has its own built-in defense mechanisms which do not permit the reader to stray too far from Jewish thoughts and associations. The constant use of Jewish material keeps reminding him of his own religious literature. It is the Hebrew language, then, that enables the reader to move on two different levels at the same time. Like a symbolic tale which can proceed in two directions simultaneously once its secrets are unlocked, so does the Arthurian romance in Hebrew. The eye of the Jewish reader notes the Arthurian tale, but through the counterpoint of biblical allusions he is continually reminded of scriptural passages. Hence the text and the language interact to a degree in polyphonic fashion.

The scribe's careful use of language is not only evident in his ability to create the image of biblical scenes in the midst of Arthurian narrative. Through the simple process of linguistic interchange, he also manages to convert Christian ideas and concepts into Jewish ones. A good example of ideational transplanting occurs when Artus says that Zinevra is so beautiful that "even the saints are amazed at it".[46] Actually, Hebrew does not possess the concept of "saint" as it is known in the Catholic Church. Hebrew,

[44] Tr., p. 13.   [45] Tr., p. 11.   [46] Tr., p. 31.

of course, does have the root for "holy" which appears in innumerable forms, and so the scribe uses "the holy ones" (Kedoshim). But since this word is laden with uniquely Jewish connotations, the original is not really translated, but transformed.

The same process appears in the scene of Lancelot's repentance after his visit to the confessor.[47] For lack of a term in Hebrew to describe the Christian concept of penance, the scribe uses the Hebrew equivalent for repentance (teshuvah), a term he has already used in his apology.[48] According to Judaism repentance mainly encompasses a change of heart, does not involve any form of punishment imposed by a confessor, and does not necessitate any human intermediary. *Teshuvah* is the Jew's path to an improved state of being by means of decisions he makes himself.[49]

The passage describing Lancelot's trip to his confessor is the only overtly Christian reference in the entire translation. However, the use here of a basically Jewish term, *teshuvah*, to describe a Christian one highlights a Jewish concept. For although in the narrative Lancelot undergoes Christian penance, the language provides the veneer of a Jewish form of repentance. And one might almost imagine a medieval reader saying at this point: "After what Lancelot has done, *teshuvah* is his only recourse." Since the scribe has already mentioned in the apology that the main purpose of his translation is that sinners "learn the paths of repentance" (*teshuvah*),[50] the use of the word here reminds the reader of the moralistic goal of the romance.

Conscious transformation of Christian concept also takes place when the Hebrew author wants to describe the Grail. In calling it *tamchuy*,[51] he has removed all Christological connotation from the traditional dish. The *tamchuy* was a plate or dish upon which food was placed for distribution to the poor, and there are many references to it in the Talmud.[52] It is possible that the scribe understood the significance of the Grail; therefore his judaization of the term and the lack of a gloss to explain it. But whether his readers knew

[47] Tr., p. 27.   [48] Tr., p. 13.
[49] See Mishna Yoma 8:8, Avoth 4:11; also Maimonides, *Teshuvah*, I, 1 and II, 2.
[50] Tr., p. 13.   [51] Tr., p. 25.
[52] Mishna Peah 8:7, Pesachim 10:1, Baba Bathra 8b.

of the Grail quest through other romances, or through oral tradition, is difficult to determine. The significant point is that in calling it *tamchuy*, i.e., a distinctly Jewish plate, rather than by any other more 'neutral' Hebrew term for vessel or dish, the scribe again heightened Jewish, and camouflaged Christian, tone and meaning.

The words that the Hebrew scribe used were not always premeditated. Quite often he had to use a certain biblical expression, for instance to describe the "coat of mail"[53] (shiryon), for lack of any other. Nevertheless, Goliath's coat of mail comes immediately to mind. But we must not confuse intention with result. Whatever the scribe's intention may have been, certain words had to elicit certain responses in the mind of the Hebrew reader.

Whether from the point of view of language or treatment, a Jewish atmosphere hovers over the Arthurian romance as rendered in Hebrew. Each of the allusions contributes to a montage effect: biblical scenes blend with Arthurian ones; or, in another figure, the Hebrew reader sees the Arthurian tale through biblical spectacles. During the jousts he might remember his own people's ancient victory; during Uter's feast, he recalls Ahasuerus celebrating and the festival of Purim; the Maid standing before Lancelot is transformed into Esther before the King; a description of the Maid's burning desire for Lancelot contains the seeds of a sermon against promiscuity. These and other situations demonstrate how a Christian romance can be judaized both in idea and content through careful use of the Hebrew language and made acceptable even to a reluctant Hebrew reader.

[53] Tr., p. 47.

5

Jewish Aspects of
Some Arthurian Motifs

A. *Channels of Transmission*

An unexplored area of critical investigation is the possible influence of Jewish writings, particularly stories and themes from the Old Testament and the Midrash, upon some parts of Arthurian romances. Eloquent testimony in support of this possibility are the many biblical and post-biblical parallels to Arthurian themes, which suggest the presence of yet another stream in the many tributaries which make up the sources of Arthurian literature.

However, before presenting Jewish parallels to Arthurian themes, some indication of cultural transmission must be provided. This is admittedly a difficult task. It would be very pleasing to report the existence of Arthurian manuscripts with Jewish glosses; or possess the testimony of writers who admit to being influenced by Jewish tales. Unfortunately, this is not the case. For lack of documentation much of the argument must depend upon a probability fortified by strong circumstantial evidence.

The first step in support of the hypothesis that the writers of romance may have utilized material from the Old Testament and the Midrash in some of their stories is to adduce the availability of this Jewish literature to the Christian writers. The second part of this procedure is to attempt to deduce the manner in which this material was used.

Comment on the presence of the Old Testament among Christians is superfluous, since the Jewish Bible was incorporated into Christian Holy Writ. Mandatory, however, is a statement explaining how midrashic material came into the hands of Christians. The contact between the Church and Jewish material goes back to the early period of Christianity. The Church Fathers themselves were the progenitors of a tradition of intellectual contact between Christians and Jews which has flourished almost continuously ever since. The Fathers showed by example that Christians might have Jewish teachers and even learn from, and quote, the rabbinic tradition.

An early Church Father, Origen (185-254), was a student of Hebrew. A resident of Palestine during the last twenty-five years of his life,[1] he not only consulted contemporary Jews for his writings, but also made use of rabbinic exegesis.[2] Ephraem (d. 381) included Jewish traditions in his writings, as did Chrysostom (345-407), whose works are also influenced by midrashim.[3] The Church Father who had the closest contact with Rabbis and their mode of interpretation was Jerome (340-420). As a result of his Hebrew studies, his commentaries contain direct borrowings from rabbinic sources.[4]

The store of Jewish material in the Church Fathers is voluminous. In his *Legends of the Jews* Ginzberg refers to about one thousand instances where Church Fathers utilized standard midrashic material.[5] In fact, some legends and exegeses which appear in Jewish works for the first time in the seventh or eighth century had already been transmitted as Jewish tradition by the Church Fathers from the third through the fifth centuries.[6]

What the Midrash was to the Church Fathers, Rashi[7] (1040-1105) was to the medieval Christian exegetes and scholars. The works of Rashi are considered the classical Hebrew commentaries on the Bible and the Talmud. By the time Rashi died, his lucid ex-

---

[1] Herman Hailperin, *Rashi and the Christian Scholars*, Pittsburgh, 1963, p. 7. Future references will be abbreviated to "Hailperin."

[2] Beryl Smalley, *The Study of the Bible in the Middle Ages*, New York, 1952, p. 13. Future references will be abbreviated to "Smalley." For a list of midrashic material utilized by Origen and Ephraem see article "Church Fathers" by S. Krauss in *Jewish Encyclopedia*, vol. VI, New York, 1903, pp. 82-83. There Krauss also states that the midrashic elements found in Jerome would fill volumes.

[3] Hailperin, p. 7.   [4] Smalley, p. 21.

[5] See Louis Ginzberg, *Legends of the Jews*, Phil., 1925, vols. V and VI, and especially vol. VII, pp. 586-598, where an index of passages is provided.

[6] *Ibid.*, vol. V, p. ix.

[7] The initials of *R*abbi *Sh*lomo *I*tzhaki, of Troyes, France.

plication of the Pentateuch had become so popular that it was considered "a household book throughout the Jewish communities."[8] An encyclopedia of midrashic statements, Rashi's text cites various sources and thereby gives even an average Jew unfamiliar with the complexities of Talmud and Midrash a rich compendium of rabbinic lore.

However, the popularity of biblical exposition was not limited to Jews. During the eleventh and twelfth centuries not only did monks and priests study the Bible, but even Christian laymen became interested in Scripture. Women too attended lay gatherings and were taught to read the Bible, which was translated for them from the Vulgate into the vernacular.[9]

The more sophisticated devotees of biblical scholarship extended their horizon to Jewish material. Christian exegetes of the twelfth century borrowed from the commentaries of Rashi and his successors, receiving their information from disciples of the Rashi school of exegesis and from lay Jews familiar with the Rashi text.

One center where this interest in biblical studies manifested itself was the Abbey of St. Victor at Paris. One of the monks there was the exegete Hugh, a teacher at the abbey from 1125 until his death in 1141.[10] He consulted Jews of the Rashi school of exegesis on their biblical texts and traditions, and learned from them several midrashic explanations.[11] Another teacher and exegete at St. Victor who had contact with Jews was Andrew. A disciple of Jerome, both in his approach to biblical exegesis and his relations with Jews,

[8] Hailperin, p. 103. Since there was spiritual alignment and communication between early English Jewry and the Jews of Rhineland and Northern France, Rashi was known by all these Jewries (See p. 273). Even in modern times most printed editions of the Pentateuch contain the accompanying Rashi text; and every volume of the Talmud includes a column of Rashi's commentaries.

[9] *Ibid.*, p. 24. [10] Smalley, p. 85.

[11] *Ibid.*, pp. 103-104. Hugh quotes three explanations by Rashi's grandson, Rashbam (*R*abbi *Sh*muel *b*en *M*eir), one of his contemporaries. Rashbam states in his commentary on Exodus 1:15 that the midwives were Hebrews; in Exodus 3:22 that the gold and silver vessels borrowed by Jews from their Egyptian neighbors were outright gifts; and in Exodus 4:10 that Moses' slowness of speech referred to his ignorance of Egyptian, since he fled from the land when still a youth. See *Commentary to the Pentateuch*, ed. David Rosen, Breslau, 1881.

Andrew was familiar with Hebrew,[12] learned the Rashi method of literal exegesis from the Jews,[13] and made constant use of Josephus, who is himself rich in midrashic material.[14] Andrew's biblical commentary was completed by 1147.[15]

Because of his interest in Jewish learning, Andrew was accused of judaizing by his colleague Richard, who disapproved of the legendary (i.e., midrashic) elements in Andrew's interpretations.[16] Nevertheless, there was wide proliferation and acceptance of Andrew's manuscripts, some of which even reached as far as the Rhineland and Austria. The earliest copy of his work is a mid-twelfth century manuscript from Beaupre. The *explicit* to this commentary on the Heptateuch describes the book as being extracts from the Fathers, Josephus, and the traditions of the Jews.[17]

The custom of biblical scholars consulting Jews was current in the Paris schools as well as in the cloisters. Three masters at the Paris schools in the latter part of the twelfth century – Peter Comestor (d. 1169), Peter the Chanter (d. 1197), and Stephen Langton (d. 1228)[18] – used Andrew's Heptateuch and quoted him in their

---

[12] Smalley, p. 155. It is also interesting to note that a General Council of the Church at Vienne, 1311, ordered the establishment of chairs of Hebrew at the universities of Oxford, Paris, Bologna, and Salamanca. Hebrew was studied and taught in the Dominican order in the 13th century. (I am indebted to Professor Louis Schoffman for the above information.)

[13] *Ibid.*, p. 163. In addition to his own Christian interpretation of "a virgin shall conceive" in Isaiah 7:14, Andrew cites the Jews quoting Rashi's interpretation that the prophecy refers not to the distant but to the immediate future (p. 163). Commenting upon "a star shall rise out of Jacob," Andrew quotes Rashi's grandson, Rashbam, who says that this refers to the Jewish Messiah; Andrew adds that the Jews say that this Messiah will do wonders (p. 160). As for Andrew's personal knowledge of Jews, in his commentary on I Kings 9:13 he says that the Jews customarily say a blessing before partaking of food; and in commenting upon I Kings 3:17, he states that Jews often use circumlocutions or direct opposites for words describing adversity or disease (p. 154).

[14] *Ibid.*, p. 126.   [15] *Ibid.*, p. 112.   [16] Smalley, pp. 156-157.

[17] *Ibid.*, pp. 175-176.

[18] *Ibid.*, p. 197. Hailperin conjectures that Comestor, having been born in Rashi's home town of Troyes, a rather small place, very likely knew some of Rashi's descendants, and that Comestor, of all other scholars, was in closest personal touch with Rashi's disciples. (See Hailperin, p. 111).

commentaries,[19] and Peter the Chanter based some of his comments on discussions with contemporary Jews.[20]

The contemporary Jews consulted by Paris scholars and monks were doubtless of the famous talmudic academies of Paris, a city famed as a center of Jewish learning from the eleventh century. Rashi's works, too, were readily available, as were other midrashic works, for disciples of Rashi and some of his descendants headed the Paris academies.[21]

Scholarly relations between Christians and Jews were not limited to Paris. The Benedictine monk, Siegebert of Gemblous, who taught at Metz (c. 1070) is said to have known Hebrew. He maintained contact with Jewish scholars and was beloved by the Jews of the city.[22] Another monk who had some knowledge of Hebrew and sought the instruction of Jews was Nicholas Manjacoria (d. 1145) of Trois Fontaines. In his works Nicholas made references to Jewish traditions, utilized Rashi's interpretations and had access to a library of Hebrew books.[23] Personal communication with Jews, however, was not the sole means for learning Hebrew. Even in the twelfth century independent study could be pursued, as is testified to by the existence of several Latin-Hebrew glossaries prepared by Christians of that century.[24] The acquaintance of clerics with Hebrew was evidently not an isolated phenomenon. During a disputation at Paris in 1240 the noted leader of Parisian Jewry, Rabbi Jehiel, remarked that the Jews taught Scripture to the Christians because there were so many priests who knew how to read a Jewish book.[25]

In summation, then, the Hebrew biblical text and its traditional commentaries went hand in hand. Those who sought to know the

---

[19] Smalley, p. 199.

[20] *Ibid.*, p. 234. In his commentary to Isaiah 7, the Chanter gives the interpretation of "the Jews of our time" concerning verse 14. In another passage, he calls contemporary Jews "hair-splitting logicians" (p. 235).

[21] See article "Paris" by L. G. Levy, in *Jewish Encyclopedia*, vol. 9, New York, 1905, p. 529.

[22] M. Liber, *Rashi*, Philadelphia, 1929, p. 129. See also Smalley, p. 79.

[23] C. Singer, "Hebrew Scholarship in the Middle Ages among Latin Christians," in *The Legacy of Israel*, eds. E. R. Bevan and C. Singer, Oxford, 1927, p. 293. See also Smalley, pp. 79-81.   [24] *Ibid.*, p. 294.

[25] H. Hailperin, "The Hebrew Heritage of Medieval Christian Biblical Scholarship," *Historia Judaica*, vol. v, 2 (Oct. 1943), p. 139.

Bible were perforce introduced to midrash, either through personal consultation with contemporary Jews who had both oral and written traditions, or by dipping into the ancient midrashim as transmitted by the Church Fathers or as quoted by the then modern Rashi and his disciples.

Now that Christian knowledge of midrash and intellectual contact between Christians and Jews have been cited, we are in a position to evaluate the significance of the parallels found between the Arthurian material and Jewish sources. Many of the parallels listed below have such a striking resemblance to their respective Arthurian motifs that some Jewish influence, either direct or indirect, must be taken into consideration.

A Hugh or an Andrew tutored by Jews of Paris may have heard many more midrashim and bits of exegesis than he made use of. These tales, then, did not necessarily have to be spread by Jews alone. Christians could very well have aided in the diffusion. When Rabbi Judah of Paris (1166-1244), a younger contemporary of Andrew, prohibited the Jews from reading "tales of battles written in the vernacular,"[26] he presumably saw romances or tales being read in Paris and attempted to halt the trend. The very same Jews of Paris who were reading French tales and fell under the ban, may have been the ones to provide the Christian writers with some Jewish legends. Here we may even conjecture some intellectual partnership: the Jews relating their stories with David as hero, and the Christians converting these tales, combining them with other elements at hand, and then giving the Jews back their David in Arthurian dress.

The noted Arthurian scholar Eugene Vinaver speculates that an "architect's" literary workshop was responsible for the *Lancelot*, *Queste*, *Mort Artu* trilogy. He assumes that it was written by this anonymous architect, and completed by two other writers, and that one of these authors had attended the abbey school of Clairvaux, near Troyes.[27] Perhaps these assumptions can be carried one step

[26] Tosafot Sabbath, 116 b.
[27] *Arthurian Literature in the Middle Ages*, ed. R. S. Loomis, Oxford, 1959, pp. 316-317. Vinaver comes to this conclusion on the basis of Cistercian coloring in the Queste. Further references to this work will be abbreviated to "Loomis, *ALMA*".

further. Just as the Abbey of St. Victor was a storehouse of midrashic information, especially that of the Rashi school of exegesis,[28] so the Abbey school of Clairvaux, with its proximity to Rashi's Troyes, could in all likelihood have been a place where midrashic traditions were easily available to the anonymous author.[29] Moreover, since a famous rabbi stated in 1240 that many priests knew Hebrew, it would not be too presumptuous to ascribe the possibility of some knowledge of Hebrew to the "architect" or his two associates, whose works are generally considered to have been completed between 1215 and 1230.[30]

The abbey at Clairvaux, where St. Bernard (d. 1153) flourished, also had a history of familiarity with scriptural study and exegesis.[31] No stranger himself to biblical exposition, Bernard gained fame for his mystical interpretation of the Song of Songs.[32] The fact that the commentaries of Andrew of St. Victor, so laden with Jewish exegesis, were read by Cistercians – four of their libraries possessed copies of his work[33] – would also presuppose some familiarity with midrashic tradition, some of whose legends could conceivably have found their way into the romance.

However, the learned Christians were not the only ones who knew of Jewish legends and stories. Whereas written material was available to scholars, the average, unlettered Christians no doubt had access to oral tales. Just as the strolling minstrels helped in the oral diffusion of Arthurian legends,[34] so the Jews carried with them wherever they went an entire body of oral tradition. Given the fact that, aside from crusades and sporadic outbursts, personal relationships between Jews and Christians were, on the whole, friendly until

---

[28] Hailperin, "Hebrew Heritage", p. 139, believes that the Abbey undoubtedly possessed a ms. collection of the Rashi school.
[29] The presence of a famous ecclesiastical school in Troyes could have been a meeting place between Jews of Troyes and Christian scholars of Clairvaux. See Hailperin, Rashi, p. 24.
[30] Loomis, ALMA, p. 317.
[31] Hailperin, p. 24.
[32] Smalley, p. 249.
[33] Smalley, p. 179.
[34] Loomis, ALMA, p. 60.

approximately the end of the twelfth century,[35] we can assume that unscholarly Christians also had opportunity to hear some Jewish legends. Jews and Christians visited and drank wine with one another, and exchanged gifts on holidays.[36] Jews even had Christian housemaids and servants on the Sabbath.[37] In such close relationships there seems to have been ample opportunity for the Jew to exchange stories with his Christian friends and thus add to the stream of oral folklore. These Jewish legends could then have spread among the Christians until they reached the fecund imagination of some cleric-author who subsequently may have utilized the motifs in his compositions.

The point of these speculations is to attempt to combine them with some basic facts. During the twelfth and early thirteenth centuries, at the very time the romances were being formulated and written by cleric-authors, there was a renewed interest in biblical study and exegesis; there was a diffusion of Jewish midrashic material, available from the Church Fathers, the Christian exegetes, the writings of Rashi of Troyes, and from oral sources; there was geographic proximity between Jewish centers of exegesis and Christian ones; there was intellectual contact between Christian and Jew and some knowledge of Hebrew among the clergy.

When all these facts are juxtaposed with the similarity of an imposing number of Arthurian themes, particularly the Arthur-David and Tristan-David nexus,[38] to Jewish ones, then the plausibility of some influence of Jewish matter upon Arthurian tradition becomes apparent.

B. *Biblical Parallels*

The chapter devoted to the Jewish aspects of the Hebrew Arthurian romance was necessarily limited to the apology and the two episodes

[35] Israel Abrahams, *Jewish Life in the Middle Ages*, Philadelphia, 1958, p. 399. Urban T. Holmes, Jr., *Chretien, Troyes and the Grail*, Chapel Hill, 1959, p. 51, states that in the twelfth century Jews and Christians lived in fellowship and had intellectual contact in Troyes and the neighboring communities.
[36] Abrahams, p. 425.   [37] *Ibid.*, p. 157.
[38] Approximately half of the archetypal patterns listed below deal with David.

included in the translation; however, the discussion of Jewish parallels to Arthurian motifs goes beyond the Hebrew scribe's two Arthurian tales and extends to various romances in the entire Arthurian tradition. Studies of Arthurian sources have concentrated on Celtic tradition and also cited some stories from other literatures, often at a loss to explain channels of transmission. Scholarship, moreover, has for the most part neglected an entire body of Jewish material which was available to the romance writers and for which the channels of transmission are no mystery. The purpose, then, of the parallels offered below is to show that Jewish story material should be added to the list of sources which critics have traditionally cited for Arthurian legends.[39]

Although sources for various legends will be discussed below in the presentation of Jewish parallels, the following general conclusions should be mentioned. Elements of the Arthurian tradition have been ascribed to Celtic stories, wandering minstrels, historians,

---

[39] An interesting exposition of Jewish parallels to the grail theme, based on biblical and midrashic motifs, may be found in Urban T. Holmes, Jr., *A New Interpretation of Chretien's Conte del Graal*, Chapel Hill, 1948. His view is that the Grail Castle represents the Temple in Jerusalem, and that the grail, the lance, the blood and the silver plate symbolize, respectively, the vessel of manna, Aaron's rod, the blood of the sacrifice made by the High Priest and the tablet of Law (p. 13). Furthermore, Holmes feels that Chretien himself was a converted Jew (p. 29). (For an elaboration of this view, see Chapter 3 in his Chretien, *Troyes and the Grail*, Chapel Hill, 1959.) However, Chretien did not necessarily have to be Jewish to know oral tradition, says Holmes. Since Chretien lived in Troyes, home of a world famous rabbinic school since Rashi's time, the knowledge of Jewish tradition could be assumed (p. 30).

Helen Adolf, *Visio Pacis: Holy City and Grail*, Pennsylvania State Press, 1960, also sees some Jewish parallels in the grail story. She likens the desire for finding the True Cross to the Jews' desire for finding the Ark of the Covenant (p. 86), the two chandeliers as accessories to the grail to the Menorah (Candelabrum) of the Temple (p. 30), Wolfram's grail stone to the Hebrew *Even Shatiya* (Foundation Stone) at Jerusalem, the maimed Fisher King to the Hebrew tradition of an ailing Messiah (p. 150), and the grail with the Jewish notion of the *Shekinah*, the Divine Presence, in exile (p. 156).

The fact that two scholars have seen Jewish parallels in such a basically Christian tale perhaps lends some support to the theory propounded herein that Jewish themes may have influenced some of the Arthurian motifs.

lais and classical myths.[40] For the Tristan legend Celtic traditions, folk tales, Arabic romance and oriental tales have been variously cited.[41]

However, with the exception of one article, no study has as yet focused attention on Jewish story matter. As the discussion of possible channels of transmission has attempted to show, we must recognize the omnipresence and availability of the Jewish themes among Christian scholars and laymen, in the form of texts and oral traditions expounded by Jews; and of the possible predilection of the cleric-authors of romance for utilizing scriptural motifs.

At variance with the European (and some Oriental) material cited as sources for Arthurian matter is the information in an article by Moses Gaster published more than seventy-five years ago.[42] Gaster seeks to accent Jewish parallels to Arthurian motifs and contends that since Geoffrey of Monmouth and Wace and Chretien were all prelates and their knowledge principally theological, they would naturally be steeped in biblical material. Therefore it is reasonable to assume that David and his deeds served as one of the models for the adventures of Arthur. According to Gaster, the basic similarities are that David, like Arthur, is renowned as a giant-killer, participates in various exploits with a group of loyal retainers, and later has a son who rebels unsuccessfully against him. The scholar does not elaborate on this thematic affinity, for he feels that the reader can pursue the remaining parallels independently.[43]

---

[40] See J. D. Bruce, *The Evolution of the Arthurian Romance*, Gloucester, 1958, Vol. I, chaps. I and II. Further references to this volume will be abbreviated to "Bruce."

[41] See Loomis, *ALMA*, pp. 122-133.

[42] Moses Gaster, "Jewish Sources of and Parallels to the Early English Metrical Romances of King Arthur and Merlin," in *Publications of the Anglo-Jewish Historical Exhibition*, London, 1887. Gaster's title is somewhat misleading, for he does not mention any romances or poems but speaks in broad terms about some Arthurian motifs and Jewish antecedents without citing sources. Future references will be abbreviated to "Gaster."

[43] *Ibid.*, pp. 238 ff. Gaster also offers some midrashic parallels which will be listed below.

At this point mention must be made of the opposing view of C. S. Northup, "King Arthur, the Christ, and Some Others," *Studies in English Philology...* *in Honor of Frederick Klaeber*, eds. Kemp Malone and Martin B. Ruud,

The Jewish story material which I cite below contains elements parallel to Arthurian motifs and is drawn from the Bible and from the post-biblical midrashic literature. The parallels are subdivided into three sections: the first deals with biblical motifs, the second with midrashic motifs, and the third with Jewish parallels to various themes in the Tristan story.

Although some of the suggested parallels are remarkably similar, we cannot always expect exact correspondence between a Jewish and an Arthurian motif, for the Christian writers were neither re-writing the Bible nor incorporating midrashim word for word. Using the ideas as a springboard for their imagination, they may have adapted and converted some of the Jewish themes to the traditional material at their disposal.

The first of the Arthurian motifs for which a biblical parallel can be cited is the one concerning the seduction of Igerna by King Uther Pendragon. The king falls in love with the beautiful married woman, desires her and lies with her. After Igerna's husband, the

Minneapolis, 1929, pp. 309-319. Interestingly enough, Northup begins by saying that the transformation of the soldier Arthur to the great king may have been inspired by the Jewish conception of the Messiah, who like Arthur had divine and human attributes. Northup then draws upon Arthurian material from Geoffrey, Malory, Layamon and Welsh literature and cites various parallels which appear in the New Testament, Christian apocryphal literature and oral tradition. Northup also cites some parallels between Arthur and Buddha and Zarathustra. Some parallels, I believe, are plausible, such as the Star of Bethlehem which appears to announce the birth of Jesus (Luke 2:8-14) and the comet over Winchester which announces Uther's successor (Geoffrey, VIII, 14, 15). On the other hand, there does not seem to be any parallel at all when Northup cites the marvels concerning the youth of Jesus as told in the Infancy of Jesus and compares this element of Jesus' character to Arthur's sweet temper which gained him universal love (Geoffrey IX, 1); Northup also cites as a parallel Jesus' miracles and victory over devils with Arthur's fight with the giant of Mont St. Michel (Geoffrey X, 3), whereas here the David-Goliath motif seems closer.

It is my opinion that the Christian cleric-authors may have utilized some New Testament motifs in addition to Jewish story material. However, I do not believe that the romancers would consciously have utilized Jesus as a model for Arthur, since it would not have been fitting to ascribe to a Christ-figure such indignities as an adulterous wife and any moral aberrations, not to mention incest. If there was conscious artistic modelling upon a biblical figure, David could easily have been used without fear of sacrilege.

Duke, is slain in battle, Uther can marry the Duchess, who is already pregnant with the future king, Arthur.[44]

In the Bible, King David notices the beautiful Bathsheba, a married woman, desires her and lies with her. After Bathsheba's husband, Uriah, is slain in battle, David is free to marry the already pregnant widow. However, the child of this adulterous union dies. Bathsheba's next son is the future king, Solomon.[45]

A noted scholar of Geoffrey of Monmouth, John J. Parry, cites two possible sources for the Uther-Igraine episode, which first appears in the form related above in Geoffrey's *Histories of the Kings of Britain*.[46] Parry cites the classical myths of Jupiter and Alcmena, wherein Jupiter assumed the guise of Alcmena's husband, Amphitryon, and begot Hercules, and the Celtic tradition of a woman conceiving a child by a god who visits her in the shape of her husband, the king.[47] However, since Geoffrey's version differs from the classical and the Celtic analogues, Parry feels that even if Geoffrey did utilize these legends, his imagination gave them free play.[48]

Tatlock, another Geoffrey scholar, states that there is no ground for assuming the begetting-story to be of Celtic origin. He mentions a folk-tale from Herodotus (VI, 61-69) and the myth of Jupiter and Alcmena.[49] Tatlock feels that the whole story of this classical myth was not very familiar to writers in Geoffrey's day. The resemblance

---

[44] *The Works of Sir Thomas Malory*, ed. Eugene Vinaver, Oxford, 1947, Bk I, chaps. 1-3. Further references to this edition will be abbreviated to "Malory, *Works*." Since Malory is the last great exponent of Arthurian matter and more easily accessible for comparison than his scattered Old French sources, Arthurian references will be made to Malory. Moreover, in some cases there are unknown Old French sources for some of the Arthurian motifs which parallel Jewish material; other O.F. sources are still in manuscript.

[45] II Samuel, 11:2-27, 12:18-24.

[46] Geoffrey of Monmouth, *Histories of the Kings of Britain*, tr. Sebastian Evans, London, 1911, Book VIII, 19. Further references to this work will be abbreviated to "Geoffrey, *Histories*."

[47] Loomis, *ALMA*, pp. 85-86. Cf. Bruce, I, 135, who also feels that the Uther episode is an adaptation of the myth depicting the conception of Hercules.

[48] Loomis, *ALMA*, p. 84.

[49] J. P. S. Tatlock, *The Legendary History of Britain*, Berkeley, 1950, p. 316. Further references to this work will be listed as "Tatlock."

84

of Arthur's begetting to the classical story might be due to Geoffrey's adaptation of the well-known Alexander story,[50] wherein Nectabenus falls in love with Queen Olympiadis at first sight and tells her that a god will come to her in dragon form, but will later change to a man. The queen approves and that night Alexander is conceived. Tatlock's view is that this story is closer than the Hercules myth to the one of Arthur's begetting because the seduction is accomplished not by a god but by a skilled man and because the human king meets the woman he desires accidentally. However, Tatlock admits that the difference is that in the Alexander story the woman willingly lies with someone who is not her husband, whereas in Geoffrey Igerna does not willingly do so.[51]

With the statements of two scholars that invention may have played a role in the Uther-Igerna story, perhaps we may look to another area where Geoffrey could have found a source of inspiration. Since Geoffrey was an ecclesiastic[52] the Bible surely was not a closed book for him. Therefore it might be reasonable to assume that with Geoffrey's clerical acquaintance with the Bible, the David-Bathsheba story played a role in his writing of the Uther-Igerna episode. One point in favor of the biblical narrative is that in Geoffrey's version no god is involved,[53] but a king of flesh and blood who falls in love with a married woman. Moreover, the thematic outlines of Geoffrey and the Bible are closer: the husband is killed in battle; the woman, already pregnant, marries the king; a future great king is born of this union.

When Arthur's kingdom is already established, his son, Mordred, rebels against his father. However, the rebellion is unsuccessful and

[50] *Ibid.*, p. 317.   [51] *Ibid.*, p. 318.

[52] Loomis, *ALMA*, pp. 73-74. Even the deception motif has a parallel in Jewish literature. This motif and Geoffrey's knowledge of talmudic-midrashic material will be discussed below in the section devoted to midrashic parallels.

[53] Tatlock, p. 317, says that if Geoffrey used the Alexander romance he "rationalized" the god-like element. Later, p. 363, the scholar states that the meaning of Merlin's *medicamenta*, used to make Uther appear like Igerna's husband, is not clearly known. The word may refer to medicines, sorceries, dyes or cosmetics. The disguise may simply have been accomplished through the use of make-up. Tatlock states that Geoffrey is usually evasive concerning the use of magic.

Mordred is killed.[54] A biblical parallel to this motif is found in the story of Absalom. He too seeks to overthrow his father, King David, but his rebellion is suppressed and he is killed.[55] The Mordred-Absalom parallel is made more striking by a statement in the Mishna (which is incorporated into the Talmud, and is thus known by almost every educated Jew). The Arthurian story tells us[56] that Mordred cohabited with Arthur's wife, Guinevere. In Hebrew literature, Absalom, the rebel against his father-king, is also known for cohabiting with ten of his father's concubines.[57] Since a concubine was considered a wife, Absalom's crime was actually one of incest.

The introduction of Mordred as the traitor who brings about Arthur's fall in another innovation by Geoffrey.[58] The historian, who may have seen some similarities between Arthur and David, could have been inspired to develop this theme and use Absalom, traitor son of the king who cohabits with his father's wives, as a model for Mordred. Although in Geoffrey Mordred is Arthur's nephew,[59] in the *Mort Artu* he is Arthur's incestuous son, a detail which is introduced by the author.[60] In developing the theme of Geoffrey, and the incest theme hinted at by Wace (who makes Mordred Guinevere's sister, probably to add incest to Mordred's crime of adultery),[61] the author of the *Mort Artu* may have noted the David-Absalom parallels and in one inventive stroke brought the traitor-

[54] Malory, *Works*, XXI, 1-4.

[55] II Samuel, chaps. 15-18. See also Gaster, p. 242, who first cites this parallel.

[56] Geoffrey, X, 13.   [57] Mishna Sotah 1:8.

[58] Loomis, *ALMA*, p. 85. Pre-Geoffrey references to Mordred are not unfavorable. An entry in the *Annales Cambriae* for 539 states that Arthur and Medraut fell at the battle of Camlan. (See E. K. Chambers, *Arthur of Britain*, London, 1927, p. 15). There is no indication there that Mordred is Arthur's nephew or opponent. Early bardic references show that Medrawt was considered highly valorous and courteous. There are also two instances where Mordred appears as a place name, which may indicate that he was held in favorable light. (See Rachel Bromwich, *The Welsh Triads*, Cardiff, 1961, p. 455).

[59] Geoffrey, X, 13.

[60] See J. D. Bruce, "Mordred's Incestuous Birth," *Medieval Studies in Memory of Gertrude Shoepperle Loomis*, Paris-New York, 1927, p. 197.

[61] *Ibid.*, p. 202.

theme closer to the biblical tale. Another minor Davidic episode seems to be reflected in the message which comes to King Arthur stating that King Rience had overcome eleven kings and stripped them of their beards. If Arthur would not send him his beard, the country would be ravaged. Arthur dismisses this demand as an outrageous insult and refuses.[62]

This episode could have been inspired by Geoffrey's account of Lucius' demands of King Arthur that he must present himself in Rome at a certain day and that if he refuses, his dominions will be put to the sword.[63] The Bible, however, offers a closer parallel. The core of the incident, the desire to humiliate a king by means of a shaven beard, appears in a passage concerning King David's servants. Representatives of the king, they are degraded by Hanun, an enemy of David, who shaves off half their beards.[64]

C. *Midrashic Parallels*

If the contention is correct that romance writers used the Bible as a source book to supplement other traditions at their disposal, the Midrash too must also be considered as a possible source of influence. The Midrash, which explains and adorns the biblical text with folklore material, parables, legends, and a wide range of homiletic commentary, also contains themes and motifs parallel to some Arthurian legends. The cleric-romancers perhaps used both the Bible and Midrash, for if the Bible lays the groundwork, the basic themes for the Arthur-David parallels, the Midrash elaborates and adds rich detail. The midrashic parallels cited below cover diverse periods of Arthur's career, including his conception, his accession to the throne, his dying command, and his influence after death.

The first of the midrashic parallels brings us back to an incident previously mentioned. Uther Pendragon falls in love with the married Igraine and desires her. His counsellor Merlin helps him to disguise himself as Igraine's husband, and she, believing the man to be her husband, admits him to her bed. The future hero-king,

[62] Malory, *Works*, I, 27.
[63] Geoffrey, *Histories*, Bk, IX, ch. 15.
[64] II Samuel 10:3-5.

Arthur, is conceived at this time. After his birth, however, his true identity is concealed until the proper time comes for it to be revealed.[65]

The biblical story of David and Bathsheba has been cited for the motif of a king desiring a married woman, sleeping with her and begetting upon this woman, after marriage, a future king. (The fact that the first child born to David and Bathsheba dies (II. Sam. 12:15-25) is the only discrepancy in an otherwise similar motif. It is the second child (Solomon) who becomes the future king.) However, the biblical story lacked the theme of deception: a man who succeeds in lying with ٦ woman because she assumes the man to be her husband. If the Bible was the source for the Uther-Ingraine episode, a midrash could have provided the deception theme, and the author's fertile imagination could have fused both incidents.

In his commentary on a verse in Exodus, Rashi tells of an Egyptian taskmaster who desired the wife of a Hebrew slave. One night he compelled the Hebrew to leave the house and then made love to the woman, she believing it was her husband who had returned.[66]

Geoffrey of Monmouth, who relates the story of Arthur's conception, could very well have known of the Rashi commentary, for Jews lived in Oxford[67] at about the same time that Geoffrey resided there,[68] and the popular Rashi text was already known to them.[69] That Geoffrey was familiar with Jewish material can be seen from one of the stories in his *Vita Merlini*. Merlin passes through the market place and sees a young man holding a pair of new shoes and buying leather to patch them when they begin to wear out. Merlin laughs at this and later explains that the young man will neither use the shoes nor the patches for he is already dead.[70]

---

[65] Malory, *Works*, I, 1-3.

[66] Rashi, Commentary on Exodus, 2:11, quoting the seventh century compilation *Exodus Rabba*.

[67] Joseph Jacobs, *The Jews of Angevin England*, New York, 1893, pp. 4, 18, 256. See also pp. 416-422 for a list of twelfth century Anglo-Jewish rabbis.

[68] Loomis, *ALMA*, p. 73.   [69] Hailperin, pp. 103 and 273.

[70] Geoffrey of Monmouth, *Vita Merlini*, ed. J. J. Parry, in *University of Illinois Studies in Language and Literature*, Vol. X, 3, Urbana, 1925, pp. 59-61.

A talmudic parallel to this episode, which Gaster pointed out, is seen in the story where Ashmedai, the demon who helps Solomon to build the Temple, laughs when he sees a man ordering a pair of shoes from a shoemaker to last seven years. Here too the laughter is prophetic, for the man does not even live seven days. [71]

Parry states that although the incident is found in an Irish tale, the Talmud is the ultimate source. [72] Geoffrey could easily have heard this tale from a Jewish acquaintance at Oxford. This Jew could have introduced various Jewish legends to the ecclesiastic, among them the story of the Egyptian, by quoting the Midrash or Rashi.

There is another midrash which contains the element of deception; however, the roles are reversed: here it is a woman who fools a man by disguising herself as the desired girl. But more important from the thematic point of view is the fact that *one* midrash contains all the themes parallel to the stories concerning young Arthur: a man desires a woman of lower station; since the woman is forbidden to him, his desire is fulfilled by means of a deception; of this union a future hero-king is born; the child's identity remains a secret; the child, now a youth, successfully passes a royalty test; the people are surprised that a lowborn youth becomes a king; his true highborn lineage is revealed.

Jesse, the father of David, was attracted to one of his pretty slave-girls. His wife, Nazbat, frustrated his plan of seduction by disguising herself as that slave, causing Jesse to make love to his own wife. So that the father would not discover the ruse, the child borne by Nazbat was said to be the son of the slave, now freed. This child was David, but his identity remained a secret until a later, more propitious, time. [73]

This midrash also contains a parallel to an important event in the

[71] Tractate Gittin 68a-68b. See also Gaster, pp. 245-246.

[72] Loomis, *ALMA*, pp. 91-92.

[73] *Yalkut Makiri*, ed. S. Buber, Berdyczev, 1899, Ps. 118. The author of this fourteenth century compilation lists this midrash as being of ancient origin.

In the Arthurian legends, another future hero, Galahad, is born by means of deception, Lancelot, who wants to be true (in his adulterous relationship to Guinevere), is fooled into sleeping with the daughter of King Pelles and upon her he begets the perfect knight, Galahad. See Malory, *Works*, XI, 2.

life of young Arthur. In the Arthurian legend only the rightful king can withdraw the sword from the stone. Many nobles make the attempt, but no one succeeds except Arthur, who is then crowned king.[74] Since the sword leaves the stone only for the proper person, Arthur has, in effect, passed a royalty test.

For the sword motif a classical parallel has been cited which tells of the test given to Theseus to see if he is worthy of being taken to Athens. Aegeus orders Aethra to bring Theseus to a certain rock under which he has placed a sword. If the boy is able to lift the rock and remove the sword, the mother should then take him to Athens.[75]

Despite the resemblance of the Arthurian motif to the classical story, a combination of various Jewish legends may be the antecedents of the sword incident. Although the following midrash may not be considered parallel to the sword motif, it is cited because it contains the theme of a royalty test and because it is included in the *one* midrash which contains so many other parallels to the life of young Arthur. The above-mentioned midrash continues by describing a royalty test passed by David. When the prophet Samuel came to Jesse's house to anoint a king, he attempted to pour the oil upon the head of David's brothers. However, the oil remained in the horn. But when David drew near the oil flowed of its own accord and poured itself onto him.[76]

The royalty test seems to be apparent. In both tales various candidates for royalty expect to have the symbol of royalty respond to them, yet they all fail the test. The symbol responds only to the rightful king. This episode of the midrash is also quoted by the fourth century Church Father Ephraem, who in his commentary tells about the oil responding only to David.[77] Since this legend appeared in a standard Christian work of exegesis, a cleric-author might easily have been acquainted with it.

However, there is another midrash whose details parallel more closely the Arthurian royalty test than does the previously cited

[74] Malory, *Works*, I, 5-7.
[75] M. Hamilton, *Greek Legends*, Oxford, 1912, p. 35. See also, Bruce, I, p. 145.
[76] *Makiri*, op. cit., Ps. 118.
[77] Ephraem, Commentary on I Samuel 16:13 in *Opera Omnia*, vol. II, Rome, 1737, p. 165.

Jewish motif. In a midrash on the life of Moses, Jethro proclaims that he will give his daughter Zipporah to anyone who can uproot a certain rod in his garden. Kings, princes, nobles and warriors come but fail in their attempt. Moses, however, is able to remove the rod and the astonished Jethro permits him to marry his daughter.[78]

Although this midrash does not describe a royalty test, the main element here in common with the Arthurian legend is a rod that many nobles hope to withdraw to achieve a certain reward. Once again only the hero passes the test.

After Arthur succeeds in removing the sword, he incurs the wrath of the lords who are vexed that someone not highborn should rise to the kingship.[79] However, later, Merlin reveals that Arthur is not lowborn but King Uther's son, born in wedlock.[80]

The aforementioned midrash concerning Jesse and the newly-anointed David continues by relating the people's surprise at the selection of a lowborn youth as king. At this point the wife of Jesse reveals that she is the mother of David, which immediately cancels the opprobrium of being baseborn.[81]

Whereas many of the analogues, both Hebraic and non-Hebraic, contain certain elements of the Arthurian story, we may assume that perhaps the author had all of these stories at his disposal. The idea of the sword, an obvious prop to a medieval writer, may have come from the Theseus legend; the element of the hero withdrawing an object from the ground (rather than lifting the stone, as in the Theseus story) where all others fail may have been inspired by the midrash about Moses; and the concatenation of events – deception to satisfy lust, birth of future king, identity kept secret, royalty test, people's surprise at choice of lowborn youth and the revelation of his true lineage – may have been prompted by a knowledge of the midrash concerning David, supplemented by an acquaintance with the Church Father Ephraem's commentary.

Another fascinating parallel between Jewish and Arthurian legends is the fact that just as King Arthur has the wizard Merlin as

[78] *Dibre ha-Yamim shel Moshe* (c. sixth century), ed. A. Jellinek, in *Bet ha-Midrash*, Vienna, 1857, vol. II, pp. 1-11.
[79] Malory, *Works*, I, 6. [80] *Ibid.*, I, 8.
[81] *Makiri*, op. cit., Ps. 188.

an advisor,[82] so King David has an advisor named Ahitophel, whose wisdom is considered supernatural.[83]

Merlin was already a traditional personage when Geoffrey was writing,[84] and the latter took from Nennius and oral traditions the material for certain scenes. Parry feels, however, that "the rest of the Merlin story seems to have been the child of his own fertile brain."[85] If so, then Geoffrey invented the relationship between Arthur and Merlin. The inspiration of providing a supernatural counselor may have come from the talmudic statement concerning David's advisor. Since we already have evidence that Geoffrey had access to talmudic material and Jewish legends, which were presumably transmitted orally by a Jewish friend, the same source may also have told Geoffrey about the legend of David's supernatural counselor.

Shortly after the youthful King Arthur has proven himself in battle, he acquires Excalibur, a miraculous sword which, in conjunction with the scabbard, prevents him from losing blood in battle. Although ciritics agree that this sword is derived from Celtic tradition,[86] a miraculous weapon known in Jewish legends should be cited. Joab, King David's chief of staff, also possessed a remarkable sword which rendered him invincible in battle.[87]

---

[82] Malory, *Works*, I, 10.

[83] Nedarim 37 b. Helen Adolf, "The *Esplumoir Merlin*," *Speculum* XXI (1946), pp. 173-193, feels that Robert de Boron modelled Merlin after the prophet Elijah, utilising both Church teachings about Elijah and Jewish sources. She states that a Jewish kabbalistic symbol, a messianic abode known as the Bird's Nest, was used by Robert for his cage-like abode for Merlin. Miss Adolf's comparison of Elijah and Merlin is quite plausible. She shows that both did not die, both would be a witness of the last things, both are chroniclers of men's deeds and the world's history, and both appear as shapeshifters.   [84] Tatlock, p. 362.   [85] Loomis, *ALMA*, p. 83.

[86] Bruce, I, p. 87, says that Excalibur is identical with the magical sword of Fergus in the Old Irish epic *Tain bo Cualnge* (The Cattle-Raid of Colley), while J. J. Parry in Loomis, *ALMA*, p. 84, suggests that Arthur's sword was derived "more or less directly" from Welsh sources. Loomis, in *The Grail: From Celtic Myth to Christian Symbol*, N. Y. 1964, p. 18, states that Arthur's sword, which in English is called Excalibur, goes back to the Welsh Caledvwlch, which in turn is derived from the Irish Caladbolg.

[87] *Mahazor Vitry* (early twelfth century France), which quotes and earlier unknown midrash, Nurnberg, 1923, Sect. 332. See also Gaster, 242, who cites this parallel.

Towards the end of his life, Arthur orders his sword Excalibur to be thrown into the lake. An arm then rises from the water, catches the sword and vanishes into the lake.[88] This incident, Bruce believes, is an invention of the author, but he also mentions a Persian parallel wherein writings are thrown into a river and an open chest sent by God appears to save the writings. Bruce claims that since this episode is not connected with a hero's death, it has no relationship to the event in the *Mort Artu*.[89]

However, Gaster introduces a Jewish legend which has a thematic parallel to the Arthurian episode.[90] When King Jehoiachin realized that Nebuchadnezzar was about to destroy the Temple, the Jewish King went to the roof and, holding all the keys in his hand, demanded of God that he take back his keys. Thereupon, a hand stretched forth from heaven and took the keys.[91]

Neither the Persian nor the Jewish legend mentions a dying king or a sword. However, the Jewish legend does contain two motifs which are found in the Arthurian tale, and it is these motifs which seem to favor the Jewish story as a possible source. Common to both stories is destruction of a kingdom by war, and a mysterious hand which comes from heaven to take back the symbol of sovereignty.

The final and perhaps most interesting parallel seems to blend perfectly with the others concerning David and Arthur: the Jewish belief which is analogous to the motif of the return of Arthur,[92] the king who was and will be.[93] Just as the English and the Bretons[94]

---

[88] Malory, *Works*, XXI, 5.   [89] Bruce, I, 434.

[90] Gaster, p. 242, does not discuss the legend, nor does he cite its source.

[91] Jerusalem Talmud, Shekalim 6, 50a. A situation somewhat similar (but neither involving a mysterious heavenly hand nor a symbol of sovereignty) occurs in *Chanson de Roland*, ed. G. Paris, 1919, vss. 660-661, when Roland proffers his right glove to God and the angel Gabriel takes it.

> "Son destre guant a Dieu porofrit
> E de sa main sainz Gabriels l'at pris."

[92] Malory, *Works*, XXI, 7.

[93] *Morte Arthure*, ed. Edmund Brock, London, 1871, p. 128.

[94] Loomis, *ALMA*, p. 64ff. The similarity between the messianic expectations of the Bretons and the Jews was noted as long ago as the thirteenth century by Geraldus Cambrensis, and in the twelfth century by Peter of Blois. (p. 64). In her article in *Speculum*, op. cit., Helen Adolf suggests that just as Elijah is closely connected to the Messiah, so is Merlin, who expects the return of Arthur, who also represents the Messiah.

viewed Arthur as a secular Christ, so did the Jews ascribe to David their messianic hopes. Prophets living several hundred years after David consoled the people of Israel with prophecies concerning David. Jeremiah tells that in days to come a scion of David will bring justice and righteousness to Israel.[95] Ezekiel, prophesying the return of Israel to its land, concludes that "my servant David shall be their prince forever."[96] Psalm 18 records that "God shows mercy to his messiah (lit. 'the anointed') David and his seed forevermore."[97]

Jewish folklore embellished this notion and eventually saw David as the deathless king, whose reign never ceases. An oftrepeated talmudic statement reflected popular belief: "David, the king of Israel, lives forever."[98] Another midrash described David as "the first and the last of the Jewish rulers."[99] These views were connected with the hopes of the re-establishment of the Davidic dynasty in messianic times, a hope which a pious Jew expressed daily in his ancient prayers.

The belief in Arthur's return can be attributed to an extra-literary source: a belief which flourished among the Bretons and the Cornish. However, the possibility should not be ruled out that this belief may have been prompted by the much older belief of the Jews concerning their ancient hero David, whose scion would be the Messiah. In discussions between Jews and Christians, no doubt the first point of difference accented was that the Jews believed their messiah had not yet come, whereas the Christians believed he had already appeared. The Jewish point of view was presumably illustrated by various statements in their traditions concerning King David, the great king who lives forever. Perhaps a Jew long ago once asked a Breton if *he* had a king who lived forever, a monarch who once reigned and would reign in the future. The Breton's reply, based on his knowledge of a historic-legendary king, may have been the first spark which ignited the subsequent legend.

---

[95] Jeremiah 33:15.   [96] Ezekiel 37:25.   [97] Psalm 18:51.
[98] Sanhedrin 98a, Rosh Hashana 25a, and the tenth century *Midrash Tehillim*, ed. S. Buber, Vilna, 1891, chap. 5, p. 52.
[99] *Shita Hadasha* (c. ninth cent.), in *Midrash Bereshis Rabba*, Vilna, 1887, pp. 376-377.

D. *Jewish Parallels to Tristan Motifs*

The Tristan legend as told by Gottfried contains so many motifs which are parallel to those in the Bible that the similarities can hardly be fortuitous. Although research on the sources of Tristan has shown that the basic story was influenced by motifs from such diverse sources as Celtic and Arabic stories, no studies have mentioned the Bible as a possible source. However, scholars do agree that much has been added and transformed by the imagination of the French romancers. The parallels listed herein suggest that the French writers' main contribution has been in embellishing Tristan's successful youth with details from the accomplishments of two successful youths in the Bible, Joseph and David.

A biblical motif is already apparent at the beginning of the Tristan story: Blancheflor dies in childbirth after a difficult labor. The child is later named Tristan because of the sorrow with which is mother bore him.[100] (Malory, reflecting the prose *Tristan*, is closer to the biblical story, which will be cited below. In Malory, Blancheflor is assisted by a midwife, and, knowing that she is dying, the mother herself names the child for her sorrow.[101])

Concerning this episode Bruce states that the name of the hero and his tragic fate "suggested a connection with the French *triste*" and prompted the poet's imagination to invent the incident of the sorrowful birth.[102] R. S. Loomis, too, agrees and credits some "ingenious Breton" with the invention of a new etymology for Tristan, based on the similarities between his name and the adjective *triste*.[103]

Although invention and imagination may have played a role, the inspiration for the birth episode could very well have come from the Bible, which describes a similar scene. Rachel, knowing she is dying after a painful delivery, in which she is assisted by a midwife, names her son Ben-oni, the child of my sorrow.[104] The stroke of

---

[100] Gottfried von Strassburg, *Tristan*, tr. A. T. Hotto, Baltimore, 1960, pp. 63, 67. Henceforth, reference to this work will be noted as *"Tristan."*
[101] Malory, *Works*, VIII, 1.   [102] Bruce, I, p. 188.
[103] See R. S. Loomis' supplement to G. Schoepperle's study in the sources of the Tristan legend, *Tristan and Isolt*, New York, 1959, p. 578. Further references to this work will be listed as "Schoepperle."
[104] Genesis 35:16-18.

ingenuity by an anonymous Breton conjectured by Mr. Loomis leaves the door open for further speculation. If the Breton's "ingenious" etymology can be ascribed to a familiarity with the Joseph section of the Bible, we may assume that his knowledge of the Bible perhaps paved the way for further additions from the Joseph story. Indeed, the main motifs of the early career of Tristan up to his encounter with Morold are apparently largely modelled on that of the biblical hero, Joseph.[105] The biblical parallels to the Tristan story seem to show that the inventing was probably done under the inspiration of the latter chapters of Genesis. As seen by a number of incidents at the beginning of the Tristan story, the romancers may have had Joseph in mind while they were composing.

One day, while Tristan is playing chess aboard a merchant ship, the merchants, impressed by his many talents, decide to abduct him for their own gain. Eventually, they bring Tristan to the country where he will make his name.[106] In the Bible, merchants abduct Joseph and bring him to the country where he will make his name.[107] In addition to the prevalent Joseph theme, there seems to be one motif in Tristan from the book of Jonah. The ship carrying Tristan is buffeted by a tempest. The sailors interpret this as a manifestation of God's wrath because of Tristan's presence. No sooner do they decide to remove Tristan than the storm ceases.[108]

---

[105] However, some of Tristan's youthful accomplishments such as wrestling and leaping, have parallels in the lives of Old Irish heroes. Cf. Schoepperle, pp. 283-287. Another view of the childhood of Tristan, based upon various European literary traditions, may be found in Helaine Newstead's article, "The Enfances of Tristan and English Tradition," *Studies in Medieval Literature in Honor of A. C. Baugh*, ed. MacEdward Leach, Philadelphia, 1961, pp. 169-185. Miss Newstead cites parallels from the early adventures of Celtic heroes, the childhood of Havelok the Dane, especially the similarity between Havelok's and Tristan's foster fathers, a shipwrecked hero in the romance of Apollonius of Tyre, and a Celtic folk belief concerning tempests. Miss Newstead conjectures that a Breton conteur knew these stories and combined various elements in them. Although Miss Newstead's suggestions are undoubtedly plausible, it seems to me equally plausible that the unknown literary artist could have found his *enfances* theme in *one* book, the Bible, and basically in *one* character, rather than resorting to a combination of disparate elements. Future references to the above article will be under "Newstead."

[106] *Tristan*, p. 72.   [107] Genesis 37:23-36.   [108] *Tristan*, p. 73.

96

The ship carrying Jonah is tempest-tossed. The sailors finally realize that the presence of Jonah has prompted God to cause a storm. When Jonah is removed from the ship, the storm ceases.[109] Common to both stories, then, is the following theme: the presence of a man on a ship incurs God's anger and a storm ensues; only when the man is removed does the storm abate.

The Tristan story continues with the adventures of the one-time homeless youth who quickly rises to prominence in the king's court. Mark appoints Tristan chief huntsman,[110] gives him fine clothes, his sword, bow and golden horn,[111] and asks him to act as if he were king. He adds that his land, his people and all that he has shall be at Tristan's disposal.[112] When Tristan meets his step-father, Rual, after a long absence, he asks if his mother and brothers are still alive,[113] then introduces Rual to the king.[114] Mark gives Tristan the region of Parmenie as a free possession.[115]

The Joseph parallels to the above incidents are striking.[116] From the depths of the prison-pit Joseph quickly rises to success. Pharaoh gives him royal powers, second only to the king himself. He gives Joseph his ring, fine linen garments and a golden chain, and places under Joseph's charge the people and the land of Egypt.[117] When

---

[109] Jonah 1:4-15. Cf. also Newstead, p. 179, who cites the folkbelief that the sea's fury will abate upon atonement ot the guilty. Miss Newstead states that the guilty person is usually thrown overboard. This belief too seems to parallel the story of Jonah, which in turn may have been the nucleus of the superstition.

[110] Tristan, p. 86.   [111] *Ibid.*, p. 92.   [112] *Ibid.*, p. 102.
[113] *Ibid.*, p. 95.   [114] *Ibid.*, p. 96.   [115] *Ibid.*, p. 102.

[116] John H. Fischer, "Tristan and Courtly Adultery," *Comp. Lit.*, 9 (1957): 150-164, suggests that the relationship between Mark, his nephew and heir-apparent Tristan, and Isolt, wherein the woman has a liason with her husband and her lover, may have stemmed from Pictish folkways which condoned a polyandrous relationship. Fischer feels that the fact that among the Picts the sister's son inherited the throne would explain the relationship between Mark and Tristan prior to Mark's marriage. Although Pharaoh is by no means Joseph's uncle, I teel that the manner in which the Mark-Tristan relationship is expressed has a strong affinity to the biblical story.

[117] Genesis 41:37-45. For another view, see Newstead, p. 176, who compares Tristan's successes at court with those of Apollonius. Like Tristan, Apolonius is cast ashore following a storm at sea. He shows such skill at sport (Tristan, hunting; Apolonius, ball-playing) that he draws the king's attention; later that evening he plays the lyre in the palace.

Joseph's brothers return to Egypt for food supplies, Joseph asks them if his father is alive.[118] And when Jacob comes to Egypt, Joseph introduces him to Pharaoh.[119] The latter tells Joseph to choose the choicest part of Egypt and permits Joseph's family to settle in Goshen.[120]

The Tristan story now turns to the Morold episode, which contains a mixture of Celtic and biblical elements. Morold oppresses Mark's country, but there is no one brave enough to meet him in single combat because of his great strength.[121] Although he is not tested in arms, young Tristan volunteers.[122] If Morold wins, the tribute must be paid; if he loses, it is cancelled. Mark tries to dissuade Tristan, but he refuses. Morold is annoyed at his challenger's youthful appearance.[123] Tristan expresses his confidence in God and in the justness of his cause. He succeeds in single combat, slays his mighty opponent, strikes off his head and achieves a victory for Cornwall.[124]

At this point the French redactors, who may have superimposed incidents from the career of Joseph onto Tristan, perhaps now turned to David for inspiration. Although there are many references to heroes playing the harp in Old Irish tradition,[125] the fact that the young hero Tristan plays the harp for the king[126] was perhaps suggested by David harping before King Saul.[127] Very possibly the French saw the David-Goliath theme inherent in the Tristan-Morold encounter and followed up the Mark-Tristan conflict with other David parallels, based on the David-Saul conflict. Given the initial similarity, perhaps the thirty knights that Tristan has as comrades[128] are modelled after the thirty strong men that David has as companions.[129]

In her study of the sources to the Tristan story, Miss Schoepperle compares Tristan and Morold to Hugh and the Formorians, who

---

[118] Genesis 43:26.   [119] Genesis 47:7.   [120] Genesis 47:6.
[121] *Tristan*, p. 123.   [122] Tristan, p. 124.   [123] *Ibid.*, p. 125.
[124] *Ibid.*, p. 135.   [125] Schoepperle, p. 287.   [126] *Tristan*, p. 89.
[127] I Samuel 16:16-23. In reference to the harping episode Malory, reflecting the prose *Tristan*, nas an interesting parallel. Eliot, the harper, sings before King Mark, who is angered and chases the harper out of his sight. Parallel to this the scenes wherein Saul's anger rises at his harpist David, who has to flee for his life. See Malory, *Works*, X, 31, and I Samuel 18:9-11, 19:9-10.
[128] *Tristan*, p. 104.   [129] II Samuel 23:13, 23-24.

appear in the Old Irish *Second Battle of Moytura*. Common to both the Irish tale and Tristan are the following elements: a kingdom must pay a tribute and a young man offers his services to the king; the king refuses to let the young man fight because of his youth, but the latter nevertheless undertakes the battle, slays the tyrant and frees the subjugated people. However, states Miss Schoepperle, the extant Tristan texts could just as easily have taken these elements from twelfth century French tradition and literature.[130]

Although the Theseus legend does contain the story of a young hero who slays ferocious men who terrorize the populace,[131] a closer parallel is found in the most generally available ancient text, the Bible: the David-Goliath story, so similar in many details to the Tristan-Morold encounter. Building upon the Celtic outline before them, we may assume that the French added biblical particulars to the Celtic sketch. Aside from the fact that the Irish tale itself may be based upon the biblical battle between David and Goliath,[132] the Tristan story contains more elements of the David-Goliath story than the Irish tale. Added are Morold's annoyance at his challenger's youthful appearance, Tristan's expression of confidence in God and in the justness of his cause, and his striking off the head of the slain tyrant, all of which are common to both the Bible and Tristan.

The Bible tells us that Goliath oppresses Israel, yet no one dares meet this giant warrior in single combat. David volunteers to take up the challenge. If David wins, the Philistines will submit; if Goliath triumphs, Israel must submit. Saul tries to dissuade David, but he, trusting in God and the justice of his cause, insists. David refuses Saul's armor because he is not experienced in its use. When David approaches Goliath, the latter disdains him for his youth. David slays his opponent, strikes off his head, and wins the battle for Israel.[133]

The continuing conflict between Mark and Tristan and the latter's flights are quite reminiscent of the conflict between Saul and

[130] Schoepperle, pp. 334-337.
[131] C. M. Gayly, *The Classic Myths*, Boston, 1893, pp. 250 ff.
[132] Especially noteworthy is the fact that in the Irish tale the hero slays the tyrant by killing him with one stone slung from a sling-shot, the very method by which David slays Goliath. See Schoepperle, p. 336.
[133] I Samuel 17:1-55.

David. This parallel is pinpointed in the scene where Mark's men discover Tristan and Isolde in the Love Grotto. They tell Mark, who approaches but does not harm the pair. Instead, Mark covers one window with grass and flowers to prevent the light from harming Isolde's complexion. The lovers interpret the covered window as a sign that Mark was there.[134]

For this same scene, earlier versions of Tristan relate different details. As told by Beroul (c. 1200) and Eilhart (c. 1170), Mark takes Tristan's sword and leaves his own in its place. By this exchange of swords, says Miss Schoepperle, Beroul intends to show that Mark discovered the couple but had pity on them.[135] An old Irish epic, *Tain bo Cualnge*, has a similar scene: a king's servant spies a sleeping couple and takes the man's sword from his sheath.[136] However, Miss Schoepperle concludes that since there are so many variants to the story, "this puzzling passage" (the exchange of spears) is not made any clearer. Bruce is of the same opinion, saying that the Irish story has come down in varying and corrupt versions and cannot be compared in detail to the Tristan story.[137]

Yet if we bear in mind Saul's pursuit of David, we find two scenes in the David narrative which resemble the above episode. One scene is a parallel in theme to the version in Gottfried, and another is an almost exact parallel in plot to the versions in Beroul and Eilhart.

King Saul is discovered in the cave where David and his men are hiding. David does not heed **his** companions' counsel to harm the king. Instead, he merely snips off a piece of Saul's robe to show that he had been there and had not taken advantage of him.[138] Although there is a reverse in the Saul-David roles here, from the point of view of theme the parallel is strong. Common to both stories is the unused opportunity for revenge in a cave when one man discovers his antagonist sleeping, and the visible sign of magnanimity. For Beroul's and Eilhart's versions of this episode there is a closer parallel in the David-Saul story. Once again David encounters King Saul sleeping, is counselled by his servant to slay the king,

---

[134] *Tristan*, p. 271.
[135] Schoepperle, 261-262.
[136] *Ibid.*, p. 264.
[137] Bruce, I, 172.
[138] I Samuel 24:1-12.

but instead takes Saul's spear to show the king that he could have killed him but really bears him no enmity.[139]

The French romancers did not necessarily have to depend on Celtic material for this passage. Given the similarity between David and Tristan in the Morold single-combat, the writers could have seen further similarities in the David story from which to draw.

In the scene where Tristan and Isolde are discovered, a naked sword, the symbol of chastity, lies between the lovers.[140] To explain the separating sword, Miss Schoepperle cites the old Irish tale of *Diarmaid and Grainne*, which has in common with the Tristan story the following elements: the king's trusted companion under the spell of a fatal power seduces his lord's wife, and both lovers live in the wilderness.[141] In a cave, Diarmaid always sleeps at a distance from Grainne, and one version tells of how he places a cold stone between himself and Grainne.[142] Yet Miss Schoepperle admits that the French poets modified the Celtic tradition of Tristan according to French taste, and that they may have changed the stone into a sword.[143]

The French redactors, through contact with Jews, may in all likelihood have known one of two Jewish legends in which the motif of a naked sword symbolizes chastity. The sixth century historical midrash of the life of Moses relates that when Moses fled from Egypt, he came to the land of Kush, where he served as chief of the army. Upon the death of the king, Moses was appointed as his successor and was married to the king's widow. But Moses, remembering the covenant, did not sleep with his wife, but always placed a sword between himself and her.[144] An older and perhaps more available source was the Talmud which tells that Palti, although married to Saul's daughter Michal, did not sleep with his wife, but placed a sword between her and himself. This device was used because he knew that Michal was David's lawful wife.[145]

Aside from the Joseph and David motifs there is another scene

[139] I Samuel 26:1-16.
[140] *Tristan*, p. 271.
[141] Schoepperle, p. 401.
[142] *Ibid.*, p. 430.
[143] Schoepperle, p. 400.
[144] *Dibre ha-Yamim shel Moshe*, ed. A. Jellinek, in *Bet ha-Midrash*, Vienna, 1857, vol. II, p. 1-11.
[145] Sanhedrin 19b-20a.

in the Tristan story which, I believe, ultimately stems from the Bible. In the Tristan story, Isolde undergoes a trial by ordeal to prove her innocence of the charge of adultery. In the presence of priests she swears to God that she has not been unfaithful and grips the red-hot iron. If guilty, she will be burned; if innocent, she remains unharmed.[146]

The above incident is cited by two Tristan scholars as an example of Oriental material in the Tristan legend. Helaine Newstead states that the Hindu ceremonial known as the Act of Truth was used by faithless wives to prove their innocence. The wife arranges for her lover to disguise himself as a beggar and then touch her. Then she can declare that she has been touched only by her husband and the beggar and thus escape the penalty. Miss Newstead says that this is such a popular story that it is difficult to say exactly how it reached the Tristan legend.[147] Miss Schoepperle also states that this theme appears in Oriental story books; however, she does not claim any derivation.[148]

No doubt the incident of the faithless woman, the lover-beggar's touch and the false declaration which is literally true stem from Oriental sources, but the procedure of the fidelity test evidently comes from the Bible. Whereas the channels of transmission from Orient to Occident concerning this story pose some problems, the story of a biblical trial by ordeal for a suspected adulteress was available to anyone who opened the Bible to the Waters of Bitterness test. A woman suspected by her husband of being unfaithful would be brought before the priest and, after a prescribed ritual, would swear to her innocence and then drink some water. If guilty, the water would harm the woman; if innocent, she would remain un-injured.[149] Common to both Tristan and the Bible, then, is a priest-supervised fidelity test as trial by ordeal, in which only the guilty are harmed, presumably affected by their psychological state.

Another version of the Tristan story seems to contain a closer parallel to the biblical test. As told by Malory, a horn with a unique property is sent to King Mark. No lady can drink from the horn unless she is faithful; if false, she will spill the drink.[150]

[146] *Tristan*, p. 248.
[148] Schoepperle, p. 225.
[150] Malory, *Works*, VIII, 34.

[147] Loomis, *ALMA*, pp. 131-132.
[149] Numbers 5:11-31.

Instead of the burning iron, we have here a drink which determines a woman's faithfulness; and it is precisely the ability to consume a drink which is the crux of the biblical test.

Two other incidents in the Tristan story may have biblical antecedents. In Tristan's concocted story of his forty-day sea journey,[151] the number may have been inspired by the ordeal lasting forty days, which is an archetypal number in biblical narrative. The Flood, Moses on Sinai, Goliath's challenge to Israel, Elijah in the Wilderness and Jesus in the Wilderness, all involve forty days.[152]

Another story with a biblical parallel is the one wherein Mark is fooled into sleeping with Brangane, who is a substitute bride, instead of Isolde.[153] This story is said to be a variant of a popular motif in folk tradition and ballads: the mistress' chastity is protected by the maidservant who acts as a substitute on the bridal night.[154] Depite the similarity, it is possible that a biblical story is the ultimate ancestor of this motif. Although Jacob has fallen in love with Rachel and plans to marry her, on the wedding night Leah is substituted for Rachel and Jacob is fooled into marrying her.[155] In both the Bible and the Tristan story the groom does not get the bride he expects on the wedding night because of someone's deception. If the French writers had the Joseph story in mind while inventing the episodes of Tristan's youth, they may very well have noticed the Jacob-Laban incident of a fooled bridegroom and a substitute bride and adapted it for the Brangane-Isolde episode.

Still another basic theme of the Tristan story – the tragic triangle: the heroic and talented youth who takes the wife of his king, and the latter's jealousy and pursuit of his younger rival – may be hinted at in the Bible. The Bible gives us two brief statements which are intruigingly rich with possibility. "And the name of Saul's wife was Ahinoam the daughter of Ahimaaz." (I Samuel 14:50); and "David also took Ahinoam of Jezreel" to be his wife (I Samuel 25:43). Except for five other references that Ahinaom of Jezreel was David's wife (I Samuel 27:3, 30:5, II Samuel 2:2, 3:2, and I Chronicles

[151] *Tristan*, p. 142.
[152] Genesis 7:17, Exodus 24:18, I Samuel 17:16, I Kings 19:8, Matthew 4:1-2.
[153] *Tristan*, p. 207. [154] Schoepperle, pp. 206-207.
[155] Genesis 29:20-25.

3:1), Scripture remains silent concerning this coincidence – so very striking because the Bible has few instances of two people, especially contemporaries, bearing the same name. And so, in the fact that Saul and David both have a wife named Ahinoam, we may have the kernel of a dramatic story that remained unwritten. A stronger hint that this may be so is provided in Nathan's reprimand to David, after the king had taken Uriah's wife Bathsheba: "Thus saith the Lord, the God of Israel: I anointed thee king over Israel, and I delivered thee out of the hand of Saul, and I gave thee thy master's house, and thy master's wives into thy bosom..." (II Samuel 12:7-8).

If there *was* a love affair between David and Ahinoam, originally Saul's wife and then David's, it may account for Saul's taking away from David his (Saul's) daughter Michal whom he had given to David as a wife (I Samuel 25:44). If David had presumably taken Ahinoam, the mother of Michal (cf. I Samuel 14:49-50), Saul then countered by depriving David of Michal, thereby avoiding a possibly incestuous situation where a man would be married to mother and daughter at once.

In any case, perhaps this unwritten drama, the career of the enigmatic Ahinoam, could have been the cause of the initial jealousy and rivalry between Saul and David, and the reason for Saul's pursuit of the young hero.

As we have seen, the writers of the Tristan story had recourse to the Biblical story and patterned some of the incidents of the life of Tristan after David; if so, then some keen scribe may also have noted the coincidence that both Saul and David had a wife named Ahinoam. And this could have prompted the development of the tragic love triangle story.

In her conclusion to her study of sources to Tristan Miss Schoepperle states that although the nucleus of the Tristan story was Celtic, the French romancers supplied many incidents and adapted the tale, recreating it according to their taste.[156] For instance, one of the non-Celtic episodes was the entire latter part of Tristan, encompassing the elements of the second Isolde, the unconsummated marriage, and the bride's offended brother, which is borrowed from

[156] Schoepperle, p. 471.

104

an Arabic romance.[157] In light, then, of the various Jewish parallels suggested to the Tristan story, to the various Celtic sources, the oriental motif, the French inventiveness and the Arabic story, the Bible must also be added as a source-book of inspiration for the French writers.

Miss Schoepperle admits that the Tristan narrative is "a mosaic of incidents that have been related" of hundreds of heroes in every language. The same incident told in the Scottish Highlands may tomorrow be found "recorded in a ninth century Hebrew text."[158] If Miss Schoepperle did not utilize the latter phrase as a figure of speech for a remote possibility, her remark contains perhaps an element of admirable foresight.

E. *Archetypal Situations*

The following list of archetypal situations summarizes the motifs mentioned above. Here they are stripped of identifiable Jewish or Arthurian elements; only the kernel of the motif remains.

1 A king desires a married woman whom he lies with; the husband is killed in battle; the woman, already pregnant, marries the king; a future king is born of this union.

2 A shaven beard as a sign of humiliation to a king by his enemy.

3 A king whose son rebels against his father and dies in a battle against him.

4 A drink which a faithful wife can easily consume, but which gives trouble to an adulteress.

5 A harper who so angers the king that the latter forces the harper to flee.

6 A magic sword which enables the bearer to achieve victory.

7 A mysterious hand which comes at the end of an era, in the presence of a king whose kingdom is in upheaval, to retrieve a symbol of sovereignty.

8 A man gains access to a married woman's bed because she believes him to be her husband.

[157] *Ibid.*, p. 580. This statement appears in R. S. Loomis' supplement to the book.
[158] Schoepperle, p. 184.

9   A future king conceived through a deception lives as baseborn child until the appropriate time when through a miraculous display his lineage can be disclosed.

10 Where all others fail, only the hero has the ability to withdraw an object from the earth, and thereby gain a valuable reward.

11 A royalty test, whereby the symbol of royalty responds to none but the rightful king.

12 The surprise that, despite his passing the royalty test, a supposedly lowborn youth should be crowned king.

13 The continued belief in the immortality and the imminent return of a long-dead warrior-king who will restore his nation to its former glory.

14 A king who has an advisor with supernatural wisdom.

15 A pregnant woman has a difficult labor while on a journey. Assisted by another woman as she dies in childbirth, the mother delivers a son whom she names after her sorrow.

16 The youth abducted by merchants who bring him to a land where he achieves fame.

17 The God-induced tempest, which abates when the hero is removed from the ship.

18 The youth who succeeds quickly, wins favor at court, is appointed to a high position, gets golden gifts and fine clothing, and is granted authority second only to the king.

19 Choice land given to the king's new favorite.

20 The youthful hero who meets a long lost relative; his request for the family's health.

21 The introduction of the hero's father to the king.

22 The youth who performs upon the harp for the king.

23 The hero with thirty followers.

24 The single combat challenge upon which a nation's future course depends; the hero who accepts when everyone else refuses; the youth not tested in arms discouraged from the attempts by the king. The mighty challenger scorns the youth, who expresses his trust in God and the right. The hero defeats and beheads the challenger and achieves victory for his people.

25 The forty soul-trying days.

26 The fooled bridegroom and the substitute bride.

27 The priest-supervised fidelity test as trial by ordeal in which only the guilty are harmed.
28 The unused opportunity for revenge in a cave when one man discovers his antagonist sleeping, incorporating the visible sign of magnanimity.
29 The naked sword as symbol of chastity.
30 The heroic youth takes the wife of his king, stirs his wrath and jealousy and prompts pursuit of his young rival.

The thirty archetypal situations listed above are common to both Jewish and Arthurian stories. Seen as the nucleus of a story from which biblical and Arthurian names have been removed, the suggestion of possible Jewish influence on the Arthurian matter may become clearer. In the light of the many close parallels and the previously cited intellectual contact between medieval Jews and Christians, a conclusion may be drawn that the Arthurian adventures, which at first glance seem to be so secular-Christian, actually contain an undercurrent of Jewish tales.

6

The Hebrew Romance and Its Ultimate Old French Antecedents

Although the Hebrew romance is based upon an Italian version of the Arthurian romances, the Hebrew episodes are ultimately derived from the Old French redactions. In the main, the two stories in the Hebrew follow the O.F. version so closely that there can be no doubt that the ultimate antecedents of the Uter and the Lancelot portions in the Hebrew romance stem, respectively, from versions of the prose *Merlin* and the *Mort Artu*.

However, a comparison of the Uter story in the Hebrew with the like section in the O.F. shows some basic differences. The story line of both the Hebrew Uter and the O.F. is the same, except that the latter version is much longer. Since the Hebrew scribe's Italian source is lost, it is difficult to determine whether the Jewish translator abridged the text, or whether he already found an abbreviated version. Nevertheless, there is some ground for speculation that the Hebrew scribe's immediate Italian source was already shortened.

The gap between the French and the Hebrew versions can best be appreciated by a simple comparison of page lengths. In the Hebrew version the Uter story is printed in two small pages,[1] whereas in the French redaction the same episode takes up eighteen folio-size pages.[2] In the Hebrew, moreover, some of the characters such as Ulfin, Jordain and Bartel are missing, the former appearing once as a nameless aide to Uter; time is greatly compressed; and conversations and events are shortened. In brief, the Hebrew Uter story, covering the same incidents from Uter's meeting of Igerna to

---

[1] *Otzar Tob*, op. cit., pp. 2-4.   [2] Sommer, op. cit., II, pp. 58-76.

Artus' birth, reads like a digest version of the O.F. version and, in addition, as will be shown below, rejects many details which are foreign to the Hebraic spirit.

A previous critic of the Hebrew Arthurian romance has suggested that the Hebrew scribe may have retold the Uter fragment from memory, rather than depending on a text.[3] Yet the possibility is very strong that the Uter-Igerna episode appeared in Italian in the much-shortened version, and that the scribe may have further abridged it. In support of this contention we must turn to the version of the Uter story as told by Thomas Malory.

A comparison of the length of the Hebrew Uter with the same episode in Malory[4] shows that both are equally brief. In Malory, just as in the Hebrew, the very first paragraph tells of Uter's love for Igerna, the wife of the Duke, Uter's desire to lie with her, Igerna's rebuff, and the Duke's hasty departure. War between the two men follows forthwith. Merlin then quickly provides Uter with the Duke's likeness and he makes love to Igerna, upon whom he begets Arthur. In both Malory and the Hebrew the pace is swift and the conversations are terse and to the point. Juxtaposed to the O.F. version, both Malory and the Hebrew read like a plot outline of the much older redaction.

Excluding the possibility that Malory may have condensed the Uter story, the fact that such diverse versions of the romance – a fifteenth century English retelling and a thirteenth century Hebrew translation – agree in the technique of literary economy may be significant. Malory's brief Uter story may be cited as possible evidence that a shortened O.F. version existed, and that the Italian translator, the Hebrew scribe's immediate source, also had access to a much condensed version of the Uter episode. Malory's source (one of several he may have had at his disposal) and the Italian's source may, in fact, represent two versions which stem from a common, and now lost, ancestor.[5]

From the point of view of length and compression, Malory resembles the Hebrew Uter more than it does the long O.F. There are differences, however, in detail. For instance, the gift of the

[3] Schuler, op. cit., p. 53.   [4] Malory, *Works*, I, 1-3.
[5] Some other points of similarity in approach between Malory's version and the Hebrew will be noted on the discussion of the Lancelot fragment below.

golden cup, common to the O.F. and the Hebrew,[6] is missing in Malory; and Uter's middleman, Ulfius (Ulfin in O.F.), who plays an important role in the French and in Malory,[7] is reduced in the Hebrew to a nameless officer mentioned only once.[8] The two other minor figures, Jordain and Bretel, also appear in both Malory and the O.F., but not in the Hebrew.[9] Also common to the O.F. and the Hebrew is Igerna's ignorance about who fathered Artus. In both versions Uter restrains himself and does not tell Igerna, while in Malory Uter admits that he is the father of the child.[10]

The characteristic difference between the O.F. and the Hebrew may be seen at the very beginning of both stories. After the introduction of the main characters, the Hebrew tells of King Uter's great feast, at which he falls in love with Igerna, then sends her his golden cup through an officer who is ordered to tell her of the King's love.[11] The same events, covered in a paragraph in the Hebrew, comprise three folio-length pages in the French.[12] In the latter the King meets Igerna at the Christmas festival which he has ordered to be celebrated at Cardoel. There he falls in love with Igerna, gives all the ladies presents and invites them for the next great celebration, at Pentecost (Whitsuntide).[13] Lovesickness has plagued the King during all this while and at Pentecost he again sends presents to all the ladies,[14] consults with Ulfin, who acts as an emissary to Igerna, and then sends her the golden cup at the suggestion of Ulfin.[15] The French version is rich in details and lengthy conversations showing the smitten and helpless state of the King.

The Hebrew depicts the King's lovesickness in one biblical word, and compresses the months of anguish into one day and all the long declarations and verbose exchanges into one paragraph.[16] Instead of a series of separate events, consultations, offers to Igerna and her

[6] Translation, p. 17, and Sommer, p. 60.
[7] Malory, I, 1-2, Sommer, pp. 59-61, 64-67.
[8] Tr., p. 17.
[9] Malory, I, 2, and Sommer, p. 67.
[10] Sommer, p. 74; Tr., p. 21; Malory, I, 3.
[11] Tr., p. 17.   [12] Sommer, pp. 58-60.
[13] Ibid., p. 58.   [14] Ibid., p. 59.
[15] Ibid., p. 60. In the Hebrew, the King sends the cup without anyone's advice.
[16] Tr., p. 17.

many rejections, the entire episode in the Hebrew is concisely narrated.

Despite the brevity of the Hebrew version, the scribe says at the point where the messenger is supposed to tell Igerna of the King's love: "Now these matters are lengthy."[17] Whether or not the scribe possessed an abbreviated Italian text, he evidently skipped the love messages[18] which Uter sends through the unnamed messenger (Ulfin in O.F.) because he considered them "irrelevant."[19] Still another consideration may have been the scribe's desire to preserve the resemblance between the Uter-Igerna-Duke episode and the David-Bathsheba-Uriah story.[20] A Jewish reader who may have noted the similarity between a king who falls in love with a married woman, sleeps with her, and marries her after her husband is killed in battle, would very likely have been sidetracked by the unbiblical quality of the long love speeches delivered by the King's subordinate.

Whereas time is compressed in the Hebrew version of the love affair, just the opposite is true in the battle between the King and the Duke. The insult of the Duke's hasty departure from the royal court at Cardoel causes Uter to attack the Duke's two castles. In the O.F. the time lapse between Igerna's departure and the military action is not mentioned. The Hebrew, however, states that three months passed after the King summoned the Duke to return to Cardoel,[21] after which Uter's troops made war on the Duke. Interestingly enough, Malory's version, too, makes mention of a definite time period: Uter warns the Duke that within forty days he would attack.[22] Although the numbers are too far apart to be considered a substantial point of agreement, the mention of a definite time may be another indication of the common version of the tale to which the Hebrew scribe's Italian source and Malory had access. However, the mention of a longer time period does not mean a longer narrative. The French version[23] of the attacks and the King's anguish is longer than in the Hebrew.

Other examples of the characteristic difference between the

---

[17] Tr., p. 17.   [18] Sommer, p. 60.   [19] Tr., p. 9.
[20] See Chapter 4, and II Samuel 11:2-27.
[21] Tr., p. 17.   [22] Malory, I, 1.   [23] Sommer, pp. 63-64.

prolix French narrative, with its accent on detail, and the Hebrew narrative, with its penchant for compression, may be seen in two minor episodes. In the French, Uter's lack of immediate success in the siege causes him much grief and he begins to cry.[24] This emotional outburst prompts Ulfin to suggest that Merlin be summoned.[25] Merlin then teases the King and Ulfin, taking on the appearance of a cripple and an old man,[26] before finally offering his aid to the King.[27]

In the Hebrew this lengthy episode, which is so full of tears and tricks in the French, is disposed of in two lines.[28] The first tells that the King attacked the Duke's castle for many days in vain; the second states quite directly that Uter called Merlin and asked his advice. The succinct narration makes Uter appear less desperate and less pathetic.

These latter two characteristics are also evident in Malory's version, wherein certain aspects resemble the Hebrew. In both Malory and the Hebrew Uter does not show his frustration by weeping (in Malory he is sick and angry at his lack of success with Igerna and the siege; in the Hebrew he is just lovesick); and in both versions Merlin appears quickly, whereas in the O.F. he plays pranks on Uter and his retainers and only thereafter appears to render aid.[29]

Another brief episode which highlights the difference between the Hebrew and the O.F. is the scene where Merlin works his magic. In the O.F. Merlin provides Uter with an herb with which he rubs himself in order to achieve the semblance of the Duke.[30] All admire one another's new guises and marvel at Merlin's craft. Then Uter (as the Duke), his friend Ulfin (as the Duke's friend, Jordain) and Merlin (as Bretel) go to Igerna's room. In contrast, the Hebrew does not specify the manner in which Merlin accomplishes the trans-

---

[24] Sommer, pp. 63-64. The verb is repeated several times: "commencha a plorer moult curement," "Et quant ses gens le uirent plorer," "& Ulfin... troua le roy plorant, si le demanda por quoi il ploroit..."
[25] Sommer, p. 64.   [26] *Ibid.*, p. 65.   [27] *Ibid.*, p. 66.
[28] Tr., p. 17.
[29] Sommer, p. 67, "& merlin aporta une herbe and li rois la prinst si sen froia..."
[30] Malory I, 1-2, and Tr. p. 19.

112

formation of Uter into the Duke. The fact that the wizard is effective is tersely stated: "Merlin accomplished this through his art."[31] Malory's version at this point is also similar to the Hebrew in that it does not specify the manner whereby the shape-changing was accomplished. Merlin merely announces the guises that each person will assume: Ulfius will be Brastias and Merlin Sir Jordan. In the O.F. this change of guise is reversed: Merlin is Bretel and Ulfin appears as Jordain.[32] All then proceed to Igerna's castle. However, in the Hebrew only Uter is in the room with Igerna, whereas in the O.F. there are three men present. In this scene, too, Malory's version is closer to the Hebrew than to the O.F. Malory gives no indication that anyone besides Uter is in the room. The fact that Merlin is described as coming to Uter early in the morning and bidding him to prepare for departure suggests that Merlin was not in the room.

If the Hebrew scribe worked from an already shortened Italian version, there are good reasons why he may have abridged even further. A superficial literary explanation may be that he considered love messages[33] and peace negotiations[34] irrelevant. But a more profound reason for the omissions may be based on cultural and religious considerations. As will be seen below, the French text makes mention of many Christian holidays, rites and practices, which the Hebrew scribe was obliged to omit. Understandably enough, these omissions were not mentioned by the Hebrew scribe for, while adhering to his pattern of expunging Christian elements, he could hardly be expected to announce to his Jewish audience that he had encountered Christian material and suppressed it. Such an admission would have destroyed the aura of Jewishness with which he so carefully sought to imbue the romance.

The Christian elements are scattered throughout the O.F. Uter episode, beginning with the great feast and ending with Artus' birth. The story opens with the announcement that festivals such as Christmas, Pentecost, and All Saints should be celebrated at Cardoel.[35] The first time Uter meets Igerna is at the Christmas

---

[31] Tr., p. 19.   [32] Malory, I, 2.

[33] Tr., p. 17, and Sommer, p. 60.   [34] Tr. p. 21, and Sommer, pp. 71-73.

[35] Sommer, p. 58, "toutes les festes si comme au noel & a le pentecouste & a le tou sains..."

feast; she is then invited back for the next celebration, Pentecost.[36] When Ulfin, the King's emissary, speaks to Igerna of Uter's love, she crosses herself[37] and calls the King a traitor. Later in the story, while Ulfin and Uter go to seek Merlin, they both attend Mass.[38] When Merlin offers his help, he asks them to swear by the saints that they would keep their oath to give him what he asks for.[39] Then the King brings relics and saint objects[40] and they swear. At the end of the story, after Artus is born, Merlin tells the King that he has found a couple who will swear on the saints that they will bring up the child as one of their own.[41] Antor, the guardian, then takes the child and has him baptised and named Artus.[42]

Although at first glance the most noticeable difference between the O.F. and the Hebrew romance is the greater length of the former, a closer examination reveals more than the superficial element of page numbers. A different mode of literary technique seems to distinguish the Hebrew from the French, and this technique may be based upon a combination of several factors. I have already speculated that an already shortened Italian version may have been the text from which the Hebrew scribe worked. Personal preference may have determined the excision of verbose speeches which the scribe considered irrelevant. Omission of this material may also have been prompted by literary (and cultural) necessity – the need to have the Uter story, so akin to the David-Bathsheba episode, sound as terse as the biblical tale.

Superseding an already abbreviated text, personal preference and literary-cultural necessity is the more significant element of religio-cultural disparity. The presence of Christian material may have been the chief reason for omissions and condensations. It is noteworthy that not one of the Christian elements cited above appears in the Hebrew text. On the contrary, as has been shown in a

[36] *Ibid.*, p. 59.
[37] *Ibid.*, p. 60, "Et ele lieue sa main si se saine."
[38] *Ibid* , p. 65, "Et al endemain apres messe..."
[39] *Ibid.*, p. 66, "Et Merlin iureres le vous sour sains..."
[40] *Ibid.*, "lors fist li rois aperter les reliques & les millors sa intuaires..."
[41] *Ibid.*, p. 74, "il & sa feme vous iruechent sor sains..."
[42] *Ibid.*, p. 75, "Et cil prinst lefant si le vit moult biaus & li demanda sil estoit baptisies..." and "& cil respont se tu le ueus baptisier a ma volonte & a mon los i aura a non artus."

previous chapter,[43] wherever a possibility for judaization presented itself, the opportunity was well used. The retention of a secular magical element such as shape-changing may be explained in various ways. First, since it was an integral part of the plot, elimination of this aspect would have altered the fabric of the tale. Secondly, no actual details of the black art are given: the episode is tersely described. Finally, the Hebrew reader, familiar with the Bible, might have compared Merlin's feat to the equally necromantic feat of the Witch of Endor (I Samuel 28:1-25), whereby she raises Samuel from the dead to speak with King Saul. A reader familiar with Hebrew folklore might even have thought of Elijah the prophet, who is also described as appearing in various guises, now as an old man, now as an Arab.[44] There is likelihood, then, that the reader may not have been taken aback by Merlin's prowess. In any case, shape-changing did not present as formidable a stumblingblock to the Hebrew scribe as did the presence of Christian elements.

Whereas the Hebrew Uter episode followed the outline of the O.F. prose *Merlin,* with much condensation and omission, the Hebrew Lancelot fragment is for the most part quite close to the O.F. *Mort Artu.* The kinship between the Hebrew and the O.F. versions shows that the writer of the Italian romance (the Hebrew scribe's immediate source) utilized a redaction of the *Mort Artu* text which has come down to us.

From the opening of the romance describing the return of Borz from the grail quest, through Lancelot's visit to the lord of Askalot and his amorous daughter, to the final scene of the tournament at Winchester, the Hebrew and the O.F. are, with few exceptions, in almost complete agreement.

Just as the condensed opening paragraph of the Hebrew Uter, vis-a-vis its much longer O.F. counterpart, is characteristic of the rest of the Hebrew episode, so the similarity of the opening paragraph of the Hebrew Lancelot to the like section in the *Mort Artu* is representative for the most part of the close pattern of resemblance that pervades the two versions:

[43] See Chapter 4.
[44] Cf. Helene Adolf, *"The Esplumoir Merlin," Speculum,* XXI (1946) p.184.

When Borz returned to the court in the city of Camelot from a land as distant as Jerusalem, he was received at the King's court with great honor and much tumult. And when he told of the passing of Galaç and the death of Prenzival, everyone in the court was deeply grieved. Then King Artus ordered that all the events which befell the knights who went on the Quest of the Dish should be recorded in a memorial volume. And so it was done. And that is the story of the Book of the Dish which is called *Libro di la Kesta del Sangraal*.

After this the King said to his officers: "Mark how many knights of the Table are missing from this Quest."

They found that forty-two were missing, having died in the war of the Quest through valor of arms and knighthood.[45]

Quant Boorz fu venus a cort en la cite meismes de Kamaalot de si lointeingnes terres comme sont les parties de Jerusalem, assez trouva a court qui grant joie li fist; que moult le desirroient tuit et totes a veoir. Et quant il ot aconte le trespassement de Galaad et la mort Perceval, si en furent tuit moult dolent a court; mes toutevoies s'en reconforterent au plus biau qu'il porent. Lors fist li rois metre en escrit toutes les aventures que li compaignon de la queste del Seint Grail avoient racontees en sa court; et quant il ot ce fet, si dist: "Seigneur, gardez entre vox quanz de voz compaignons nos avons perduz en ceste queste." Et il i gardent meintenant, si trouverent qu'il leur en failloit trente et deus par conte, ne de touz ceus n'i avoid un seul que ne fust morz par armes.[46]

An almost exact correspondence between the Hebrew and the O.F. is readily apparent. The only difference between the two texts is that the Hebrew adds the name of the book about the grail quest and that it lists forty-two men killed in the quest, while the French has thirty-two.[47]

The very next sequence in Hebrew, Artus asking Gawain how many men he killed, also follows the O.F., but in line with the scribe's predilection for condensing speeches, the interchange between Gawain and the King is reduced in the Hebrew to three indirect quotations and two direct speeches.[48] In contrast the

[45] Tr., pp. 23, 25. [46] Frappier, op. cit., pp. 1-2.
[47] Even in French mss. of the *Mort Artu* there is no agreement as to the number of knights slain. Although Frappier's text has thirty-two, the text edited by Sommer, vol. VI, p. 204, states that twenty-two men were slain in the grail quest.
[48] Tr., p. 25.

French proceeds in more leisurely fashion, with Gawain hesitating to answer and Artus prodding him until he finally replies.[49]

In the next major scene, the meeting of Lancelot and Guinevere, the Hebrew tells of Guinevere's sadness and tears while Lancelot was at the monk's retreat and how "strong as death" was the love she had for him. This passage is not in the O.F., but both versions continue by telling of Lancelot's reckless passion for the King's wife and of Agravain's awareness of the affair:

> And whereas he would previously kiss her discreetly and cover up his sins, he now exceeded the mark in displaying his desire in this evil matter, and she likewise, until the entire court in general and Agravan in particular preceived this.[50]

> Et se il avoit devant meintenu celui pechie si sagement et si couverete-ment que nus ne s'en estoit aperceuz, si le meintint apres si folement que agravains, le freres monseigneur Gauvain, que onques ne l'avoit ame clerement et plus se prenoit garde de ses errremens que nus des autres, s'en aperçut.[51]

Although the Hebrew lacks the statement about Agravain's dislike of Lancelot, both versions continue by telling of the Queen's beauty. The Hebrew, however, does not contain the O.F. statement that Guinevere was fifty years old,[52] but does add the moralistic and thematic note that the pair's evil desire caused all the subsequent ruin.[53]

The following episodes, Agravain informing King Artus about Lancelot's treachery and Lancelot's departure for the tournament at Winchester, are basically similar in both versions. An interesting difference in the Hebrew is the little formal love speech of Lancelot and the sentence describing the love scene between the couple.[54] Presumably this passage was found in the Italian version utilized by the Hebrew scribe. The courtly tone of the speech, so odd in Hebrew, was made even more bizarre by Lancelot's using the pious Jew's mode of reference for God, *ha-shem* (the Name).[55]

---

[49] Frappier, pp. 2-3.   [50] Tr., p. 29.   [51] Frappier, p. 3.
[52] Frappier, p. 4, "l'aage de cinquante anz..." Sommer, vol. VI, p. 205, states that some mss. do not give the queen's age. The scribe's source was evidently a version of the latter redactions.
[53] Tr., p. 29.   [54] Tr., p. 33.   [55] Tr., p. 33.

117

Other elements in the Hebrew ms. not found in the O.F. are the names given to the lord of Askalot, Lanval,[56] and his two sons, Edelpert and Karavoç.[57] All three figures remain unnamed in the extant O.F. sources. Aside from the variance in names, the scene of Lancelot at the lord of Askalot's house is basically the same in the O.F. as in the Hebrew.

The Maid of Askalot's love for Lancelot is also described in both versions.[58] The Hebrew twice represents the Maid as having a burning passion for Lancelot,[59] a description which is not found in the O.F. Such an addition by the Hebrew scribe can be considered surprising, in view of his desire to give the Arthurian romance a more moral coloration, but, on the other hand, it could well point up the moral implication. However, there is a possibility that the Hebrew scribe may have found this description in his Italian source. As possible proof that there existed a version of the romance which ascribed greater passion to the Maid, we again turn to Malory. Although the latter author does not relate some of the scenes common to the Hebrew and the O.F., such as Arthur's order to write a book about the grail quest, Gawain's sorrow at having killed Bagdemagus, or Agravain's discussion with the King concerning Lancelot's affair with Guinevere, Malory's description of the Maid is relevant because of its similarity to the Hebrew version.

Malory, like the Hebrew, tells of the Maid's love for Lancelot directly upon introducing the girl, and then adds that she was "so hot in her love" that she asked him to wear a token of hers at the tournament.[60] Whereas in the O.F. the Maid's love for Lancelot is implied in her request, both Malory and the Hebrew describe her passion explicitly at the outset of her relationship with Lancelot.

Another point of contrast between the French and the Hebrew is seen when Lancelot leaves the lord of Askalot's house. At that time Lancelot takes leave of the entire family, including the lord's wife. No mention of this woman is made in the O.F.[61] But both versions

---

[56] Tr., p. 35.
[57] Tr., p. 37, and cf. Frappier, p. 8.
[58] Frappier, pp. 9-10, and Tr., p. 39.
[59] Tr., p. 39.   [60] Malory, XVIII, 9.
[61] Tr., p. 41, Cf. Frappier, p. 11, "si s'en parti de chies le vavasor et commenda a Diue le vavasor et la damoisele..."

118

tell how Lancelot, with his companion, the lord's son, rides toward Winchester, lodging at the house of the young knight's aunt.[62]

In the French the conversation between Lancelot and the knight concerning the aunt is much longer than in Hebrew.[63] The French also contains, while the Hebrew omits, the aunt's welcome to her nephew, and the Hebrew reduces the aunt's hospitable treatment of Lancelot to one line. The order of events, too, is slightly altered in the Hebrew: first comes the kind welcome and then the aunt's question concerning Lancelot's identity, whereas in the French the aunt immediately questions her nephew and then showers Lancelot with compliments and leads him to a room with a fine bed.[64]

From this point to the scene of Lancelot in battle, the Hebrew version agrees with the French. The only important departures from the French text can be readily explained. The first is the omission of a few lines which depict Lancelot's visit at daybreak to hear Mass and say his prayers "einsi comme chevalier crestien doit fere."[65] The second occurs when the knights praise Lancelot's valor, calling his blows the most beautiful they had seen: "...et distrent aucun qu'il avoient veu un biau coup."[66] In the Hebrew the knights are less enthusiastic.[67] The scribe may have toned down this particular passage for, although a knightly battle could easily be rendered into Hebrew, the more subtle points concerning the aesthetic of the joust was foreign to the Hebraic world. Even if each word could be translated into Hebrew, the notion of a beautiful blow – the phrase itself was a contradiction, an oxymoron for the Jew – could not be appreciated and would very likely offend the reader's sensibility. A few lines later in the Hebrew when Estor de Mareis strikes down Edelpert, the knights shout: "Praised be the living God..."[68] a traditional Hebrew blessing which does not appear in the O.F. The Hebrew translator, in typically Jewish fashion, has the knights ascribe the victory not to man, but to God, to whom thanks for victory are due.

The pattern of the rest of the battle is the same in both the O.F. and the Hebrew. At the point in the battle where Lancelot's spear

---

[62] Frappier, p. 11, and Tr., p. 41.
[63] Frappier, p. 11.   [64] *Ibid.*, pp. 11-12, Tr., p. 41.
[65] Frappier, p. 12.   [66] *Ibid.*, p. 14.   [67] Tr., p. 45.
[68] Tr., p. 45.

breaks and he begins his assault against the knights, the Hebrew ms. breaks off.[69] The concluding image of Lancelot felling knights like lambs and cutting horses' throats like pumpkins does not appear in the French version.

Aside from the Hebrew scribe's additions and deletions which were prompted by religio-cultural necessity, the main differences between the *Mort Artu* and the Hebrew version are these: the Hebrew gives the title of the book concerning the grail quest, contains a brief love speech by Lancelot and a description of a love scene, adds a wife to the lord of Askalot, names the lord and his two sons, and describes more explicitly the Maid's passion for Lancelot. (Aside from the last two points – the naming of the lord and his sons and the Maid's passion – none of the above mentioned details appear in Malory.) The French also contains more dialogue, but presumably the Hebrew scribe compressed or omitted some speeches, in accordance with the statement in the apology concerning omission of some passages.[70]

However, it is possible that many of the points of divergence found in the Hebrew version and the scribe's Italian source were taken from a now lost French redaction. For example, the names of the lord of Askalot and his two sons need not have been an invention of either the Hebrew scribe or the Italian translator. Malory's version of the above details supports the contention that the names might have appeared in some O.F. version. Although the names of the lord of Askalot and his two sons are not in the *Mort Artu*, Malory, like the Hebrew text, provides names for the lord (Bernard) and for his two sons (Tirry and Lavaine).[71] At this point there is also a certain affinity between the Hebrew and Malory in a brief narrative sequence. Both mention Askalot as the place where Lancelot stays and then provide a name for the lord. Both versions, too, then immediately tell that King Arthur recognized Lancelot as soon as he arrived. This juxtaposition of detail is not found in the O.F. In addition to the fact that both Malory and the Hebrew name the lord's two sons, another noteworthy point is the similarity between the names Lanval and Lavaine (despite the fact that the

[69] Tr., p. 49, and Frappier, p. 17.   [70] Tr., p. 9.
[71] Malory, XVIII, 9.

120

former is the father in the Hebrew and the latter the son in Malory). The foregoing details suggest that perhaps Malory's source and the Italian translator's source both had a common ancestor, a now unknown variant of the traditional *Mort Artu* which has come down to us.

I have suggested that perhaps Malory had at his disposal, in addition to other material, a version of the O.F. romances which are no longer extant; and that his text perhaps stemmed from the same French version as the one utilized by the Hebrew scribe's source, the Italian translator. Malory's condensation of the Uter-Igerna episode, so similar to the Hebrew in the technique of literary compression; his diminution of Uter's frustration and Merlin's frivolousness; his silence on the details of the magical trans-formation; his indication that only Uter was in the room with Igerna; his naming of the lord and his two sons; and his ascribing of passion to the Maid of Askalot at her first encounter with Lancelot, all bear similarity to the devices and details used in the Hebrew romance, and are at odds with the O.F. texts. It would certainly be a great coincidence if both Malory and the Hebrew scribe (or the Italian translator) invented the abovementioned points inde-pendently.[72]

With few exceptions there is a general similarity between the Hebrew version of the *Mort Artu* and the French text: both contain the same order of events, conversations, even relatively trifling details. Considering the fact that we are comparing a Hebrew translation of an Italian translation of an O.F. *Mort Artu* with an extant text of *Mort Artu* which is definitely not the version that the unknown Italian translator utilized, the affinity between the Hebrew and the O.F. is truly remarkable. The agreement of the texts shows that, given some freedom to execute minor changes based on editorial decisions and, as in the Hebrew ms., religious persuasion and cultural objections, the medieval translators were so faithful to the stories they encountered that even a tertiary translated version could resemble a collateral version of its ultimate primary source.

---

[72] In his explanatory notes to his edition of Malory's *Works*, p. 1573, Vinaver cites the views of various critics that Malory's departures from the O.F. version can be ascribed to the source he used.

Bibliography

Manuscript

Cod. Vat. Hebr. Urbino 48, ff. 75-77

Abrahams, Israel. *Jewish Life in the Middle Ages*, Philadelphia, 1958.

Adolf, Helen. "The *Esplumoir Merlin*," Speculum XXI (1946), pp. 173-193.

Adolf, Helen. *Visio Pacis: Holy City and Grail*, Pennsylvania State Press, 1960.

Al-Harizi, Judah. *Tahkemoni*, ed. Y. Toporowski, Tel-Aviv, 1952.

Anatoli, Jacob. *Malmad ha-Talmidim*, Lyck, 1866.

Baer, Y. "Secular Literature of German and French Jewry" (Hebrew), *Sinai*, XVI (1953), pp. 288-298.

Baron, Salo. *A Social and Religious History of the Jews*, Philadelphia, 1958. 7 vols.

Berakya ha-Nakdan. *Dodi V'Nekdi*, London, 1920.

Berakya ha-Nakdan. *Mishley Shualim*, ed. A. M. Haberman, Tel-Aviv, 1946.

Bevan, E. R. - Singer, C. *The Legacy of Israel*, Oxford, 1927.

Bible (Hebrew), Jerusalem, 1956.

Bible (English), Philadelphia, 1917.

Boccaccio. *The Decameron*, tr. R. Aldington, N. Y., 1962.

Bruce, J. D. *Evolution of the Arthurian Romance*, Gloucester, 1958.

Bruce, J. D. "Mordred's Incestuous Birth," *Med. Studies in Memory of Gertrude Schoepperle Loomis*, Paris-New York, 1927, pp. 197-207.

Chambers, E. K. *Arthur of Britain*, London, 1927.

Chaucer, *The Complete Works*, ed. F. N. Robinson, Boston, 1933.

Chomsky, W. *Hebrew: The Eternal Language*, Philadelphia, 1958.

Denomy, A. J. "An Inquiry into the Origins of Courtly Love," *Med. Studies*, Vol. VI (1944), pp. 175-260.

Denomy, A. J. "Fin' Amors: The Pure Love of the Troubadors, Its Amorality and Possible Source," *Med. Studies*, Vol. VII (1945), pp. 139-207.

Dibre ha-Yamim shel Moshe, ed. A. Jellinek, in *Bet ha-Midrash*, II, Vienna, 1857.

Diwan of Samuel Hanagid, ed. D. S. Sassoon, London, 1934.

Ephraem. *Opera Omnia*, II, Rome, 1737.

Fisher, John H. "Tristan and Courtly Adultery," *Comp. Lit.* 9 (1957) pp. 150-164.

Flutre, Fernand. *Table des noms propres avec toutes leurs variants figurant dans romans du moyen age ecrits en français ou en provençal et actuellement publies ou analyses*, Poitiers, 1962.

Gardner, E. *The Arthurian Legend in Italian Literature*, London, 1930.

Gaster, Moses. "The History of the Destruction of the Round Table", *Folklore*, XX (1909), pp. 272-294.

Gaster, Moses. "Jewish Sources of and Parallels to the Early English Metrical Romances of King Arthur and Merlin," in *Publications of the Anglo-Jewish Historical Exhibition*, London, 1887.

Geoffrey of Monmouth, *Histories of the Kings of Britain*, tr. Sebastian Evans, London, 1911.

Geoffrey of Monmouth. *Vita Merlini*, ed. J. J. Parry, in *University of Illinois in Language and Literature*, X, 3, Urbana, 1925.

Gottfried von Strassburg, *Tristan*, tr. A. T. Hotto, Baltimore, 1960.

Ginzberg, Louis. *Legends of the Jews*, Philadelphia, 1925.

Gudemann, M. *Geschichte des Erziehungswesen und der Kultur der Abendlandischen Juden*, Vienna, 1880.

Gudemann, M. *Jews in Italy* (Hebrew), Warsaw, 1896.

Hailperin, Herman. "The Hebrew Heritage of Medieval Christian Biblical Scholarship," *Historia Judaica*, V (Oct. 1943), pp. 133-154.

Hailperin, Herman. *Rashi and the Christian Scholars*, Pittsburgh, 1963.

Hamilton, M. *Greek Legends*, Oxford, 1912.

Harris, Monford. "Concept of Love in *Sefer Hasidim*," *Jewish Quarterly Review*, L (1959-1960), pp. 13-44.

Holmes, Urban T. *A New Interpretation of Chretien's Conte del Graal*, Chapel Hill, 1948.

Holmes, Urban T. *Chretien, Troyes and the Grail*, Chapel Hill, 1959.

Ibn Sahula, Yizhak ben Shlomo. *Mashal Ha-Kadmoni*, Tel-Aviv, 1952.

Isaac ben R. Judah Halevi. *Paaneah Raza*, Tarnopol, 1803.

Jacobs, Joseph. *The Jews of Angevin England*, N. Y., 1893.

Jewish Encyclopedia, N. Y., 1901-1906.
    Krauss, S., article on "Church Fathers."
    Levy, L. G., article on "Paris."

Kalilah V'Dimnah, tr. Jacob ben Eleazar, ed. Y. Dinaburg, Paris, 1881.

Liber, M. *Rashi*, Philadelphia, 1929.

Loomis, R. S. (ed.). *Arthurian Literature in the Middle Ages*, Oxford, 1959.

Loomis, R. S. *Celtic Myth and Arthurian Romance*, N. Y., 1927.

Loomis, R. S. *The Grail: From Celtic Myth to Christian Symbol*, New York, 1964.

"The Love Stories of Jacob ben Eleazar," ed. H. Schirmann, in *Studies of the*

Research Institute for Hebrew Poetry in Jerusalem, V, Jerusalem-Berlin, 1939, pp. 209-266.

Magazin f. d. Wissenschaft d. Judenthums, ed. A. Berliner, Berlin, 1885.

Mahazor Vitry, Nurnberg, 1923.

Maimonides. *Commentary to Sanhedrin*, Slavita, 1830.

Maimonides. *Guide to the Perplexed*, tr. J. Al-Harizi, Warsaw, 1904.

Margolies, M. - Marx, A. *A History of the Jewish People*, Philadelphia, 1956.

Millgram, Abraham. *An Anthology of Medieval Hebrew Literature*, N. Y., 1961.

Mishna, Tel-Aviv, 1932.

Mishna, Eng. tr. by H. Danby, Oxford, 1933.

Mort Artu, ed. J. Frappier, Paris, 1956.

Morte Arthure, ed. Edmund Brock, London, 1871.

Newstead, Helaine. "The Enfances of Tristan and English Tradition," *Studies in Med. Lit. in Honor of A. C. Baugh* (1961), pp. 169-185.

Northup, C. S. "King Arthur, the Christ, and Some Others," *Studies in English Philology...in Honor of Frederick Klaeber*, Minneapolis, 1929, pp. 309-319.

Otzar Tob, ed. A. Berliner, Berlin, 1885.

Roth, Cecil. *History of the Jews in Italy*, Philadelphia, 1946.

Samuel ben Meir. *Commentary to the Pentateuch*, ed. David Rosin, Breslau, 1881.

Samuel ben Meir. *Commentary to the Song of Songs*, Leipzig, 1855.

Schirmann, H. *Anthology of Hebrew Poetry in Italy* (Hebrew), Berlin, 1934.

Schirmann, H. *Hebrew Poetry in Spain and Provence*, Jerusalem-Tel-Aviv. 1960.

Schoepperle, G. *Tristan and Isolt*, N. Y. 1959.

Schuler, M. "Die hebraische Version der Sage von Arthur und Lanzelot aus dem Jahre 1279," *Archiv f. neure Sprachen v. Lit.*, CXXII (1909), pp. 51-63.

Sefer Hasidim, ed. Reuben Margoliot, Jerusalem, 1958.

Shabbetai, Yehuda. *Soneh Nashim*, ed. E. Ashkenazi, in *Taam Zekenim*, Frankfurt, 1854, ff. 1-12.

Shita Hadasha, in *Midrash Bereshis Rabba*, Vilna, 1887.

Shulvass, M. *Jewish Life in Italy during the Renaissance* (Hebrew), N. Y., 1955.

Smalley, Beryl. *The Study of the Bible in the Middle Ages*, N. Y., 1952.

Steinschneider, Moritz. *Hebraische Uebersetzungen*, Berlin, 1893.

Talmud (Babylonian), Vilna, 1835.

Talmud (Jerusalem), N. Y., 1909.

Tatlock, J. P. S. *The Legendary History of Britain*, Berkeley, 1950.

The Torah (English), Philadelphia, 1962.

Vogelstein, H. - Rieger, P. *Geschichte der Juden in Rom*, Berlin, 1896.

Vulgate Version of the Arthurian Romances, ed. H. O. Sommer, Washington, 1908-1913.

Waxman, M. *History of Jewish Literature*, N. Y., 1960.
The Works of Sir Thomas Malory, ed. Eugene Vinaver, Oxford, 1947.
Yalkut Makiri, ed. S. Buber, Berdyczev, 1899.
Yalkut Shimoni, Berlin, 1926.
Yehiel ben Yekutiel. *Maalot ha-Midot*, Warsaw, 1876.
Zinberg, I. *The History of the Literature of Israel*, Tel-Aviv, 1959.